The Complete Book of Fussing and Nagging

Ben Watford

authorHOUSE®

AuthorHouse™
1663 Liberty Drive, Suite 200
Bloomington, IN 47403
www.authorhouse.com
Phone: 1-800-839-8640

© *2008 Ben Watford. All rights reserved.*

No part of this book may be reproduced, stored in a retrieval system, or transmitted by any means without the written permission of the author.

First published by AuthorHouse 2/23/2008

ISBN: 978-1-4343-6371-8 (sc)

Library of Congress Control Number: 2008901387

Printed in the United States of America
Bloomington, Indiana

This book is printed on acid-free paper.

I dedicate this book to my wife Barbara for surviving fifty-six years of my bad habits and to my children, Benita, Barry, Becky, Bevlee, Bonnie and Barbra. A special thanks goes to my daughter, Dr. Becky Vargo for reading and correcting the manuscript.

Table of Contents

My Wife's Point of View • 1
My point of view • 5
On Golf • 23
The Bathroom • 38
On Clothes And Dressing • 43
On Drinking • 50
On Sex • 56
On Writing • 85
The Office and supplies • 93
Fussing • 106
On Shopping • 119
Just Talking • 123
Who Is The Boss • 140
House Repairs • 147
Television • 153
Time Together • 160
Helping Out • 166
Looking for Things • 170
Love • 180
The Pottery Shop • 184

Around The House · 190
The Cars And Driving · 193
Organization · 201
Listening · 205
Family · 209
Life & Living · 214
Money And Finance · 229
The Bedroom · 239
Need My Space · 245
The Dinner Table and Eating · 248
Husbands · 260
Breakfast · 264
Kissing · 268
Joking · 270
Telephone · 273
Eating · 276
Greetings · 280
Doctor's Office · 282
E-Mail · 284
The Plaque · 287
Rules of the House · 288

My Wife's Point of View

Y ou can write any thing that you want to write and send it to any one that you want to. Everyone will realize that you are a blooming idiot and your elevator doesn't reach the top floor.

You men don't know what it's like to have a man around the house 24-7 with nothing to do but annoy someone.

WIFE

Fussing and nagging as an art form

My point of view

I am of the opinion, that at some point in a marriage, all wives fuss and nag their husbands. My mother fussed and nagged my father and my wife is an expert at fussing and nagging. My wife has developed fussing and nagging into a beautiful art form. I enjoy her comments about my bad habits and me. I have quite a few bad habits. We have been married for almost sixty years and I would not have it any other way. There are a few things in the past that I would change. However, I would not change my wife as she is a beautiful specimen of womanhood.

I f a woman is going to fuss and nag, it should be interesting, enjoyable and fun to listen to. It should be as beautiful as the songs of birds. It should be informative, witty and intelligent.

F ussing and nagging should be a work of art as haunting, lovely and strange as a Pablo Picasso painting. Fussing and nagging should not be used to make your mate into what you think he should be, as that my dear, is impossible. It should be something that the two of you can laugh and joke about in order to make your union stronger.

W e, my wife and I, are retired schoolteachers. We have six grown children. We retired from teaching in Smithtown and Centereach, New York respectively and built a house in Fairfield Harbour, Near New Bern, North

Carolina. Between work and raising the six children, no mean task, we really did not get to know each other until we retired and moved into a new house together. The discovery began when we moved into our new home and had to live with each other with no distractions. This is a new dilemma brought about by relatively good health through the senior years as well as longevity.

One morning I woke up and said, "Who is this woman that I am married to?"

I am sure that my wife said, "Who in the hell is this man that I now have to live and share a house with."

I am convinced that man was never meant to live with woman. The two are practically speaking from two different worlds. This is especially true when they are both retired, set in their ways, have to share a house and start to get in each other's way. Women should really live by themselves and just have men visit them occasionally.

My wife and I moved into our new home. The first thing that my wife said to me was, "Now that we are both retired and have this new house you are going to help me with the housework."

I said, "Sure, I will help you with it."

I aim to please.

The next day I went out and hired a cleaning lady. Talk about one angry wife; she called me lazy {which I am} and a few other things

not for polite company. I finally convinced her that it was the right thing to do. What with golf, my pottery business and community activities, where would I find the time for housework? What happened next you may not believe, unless you are another woman?

The day before the cleaning lady was to come and clean the house my wife said to me, "The cleaning lady is coming tomorrow; I want you to clean up your study."

I said to her, "That is what I hired the cleaning lady to do, clean the house and clean up my mess."

My wife said, and she was serious, "I am not going to allow anyone to come in my house and see a mess, a cleaning lady or anyone else."

My wife wants me to clean the house for the cleaning lady. Does that make any sense? I would like to ask {not the women of the world, they are all alike} the men out there, does it make any sense to clean the house for the house cleaner? She was hired to clean up the mess, my mess. My wife's logic, which makes sense only to other women, escapes me. Yet, I went in and arranged some of the papers on my desk into another pile and moved a few chairs just to make her happy.

I aim to please.

My wife spends much of her time fussing and nagging me about my bad habits, I have many. However, her fussing and nagging has developed into an art form. She is really good at it and I enjoy it. Not that I have any intention of changing the way that I am. Her nagging is really witty and she just seems to have the ability to make it enjoyable, funny and amusing. I hope other husbands enjoy their wives fussing and nagging as much as I do.

I really think that fussing and nagging is something that girls learn from their mothers and pass down from generation to generation. *My wife has tried many times to teach me to fuss and nag.* Finally, she just gave up. She says I do not have the knack for it. My wife says I talk too fast and move my hands too much to fuss and nag effectively. She tried to get me to talk more slowly when I want to fuss, but that did not work either. She also claims that I do not have the natural wit to be a good fusser and nagger. I have given up trying to learn to fuss and nag and just enjoy her special talent for making comments about me and the way that I am amusing.

My wife is an independent, modern woman, and a very special example of the results of the women's liberation movement of the sixties and seventies. We have always been different from most married couples. We have a special financial arrangement. From the beginning of our marriage we have had separate bank accounts. My wife has her own checking and {savings} account and I have mine. I put savings in parenthesis because she does not know the meaning of the word "savings." We started this early in our marriage when I realized that my wife only wanted to spend and spend and I wanted to save and save. My wife taught school for thirty years and never saved one dime. When she retired, her saving account had a zero balance. Her philosophy was that she enjoyed spending and if she did not spend it, when she died someone else would spend it. When we go out to dinner, she always pays for her meal and I pay for mine. When we go to movies, the theater or concert hall, she pays for her ticket and I buy mine. If she wants pop corn, she has to buy it. If I borrow money from her, she makes sure that I pay it back. When she borrows money from me, she always pays it back. While we were working, I purchased IRA's for both of us and true to form some of my children spent the money that I saved.

 She has recently taken over paying my bills for me using my checkbook and her computer. Most of them she pays on line, a thought that never occurred to me. Like everything else, my wife does, she keeps perfect records of her accounts and mine. She started doing this because she found that many times I would pay a bill twice or would pay more than the required amount, or worst of all, I would forget to pay the bill. I really never looked carefully at my bills; I just tried to pay them when they came in. My wife, with her ordered mind and ordered system, could not believe the mess that I had made of my accounts, so now she pays my bills for me out of my account. This also gives her access to my checking and saving account, so there is no need to think that when I borrow money from her I am not going to pay it back. Our financial system might not work for others but it works well for us.

My wife and I have radically different buying habits. When I go to a store and see a shirt for seventy-five dollars, I cannot force myself to buy it. I still believe that a shirt should cost $1.99. I remember paying $19.95 for a suit and it came with an extra pair of pants. I still believe I paid too much for that damn suit.

My wife, on the other hand, just buys what ever she wants regardless of the price. She has to buy my clothes because I refuse to pay today's prices. I suspect this is due to the way we grew up. I was one of fifteen children and my father owned a bicycle that he would not let me ride. My wife was one of five children and her father owned a car. I might add that they also had electric lights and indoor plumbing. I guess in some ways, I am like my father. After World War II, some of my siblings and I got together and put a bathroom in the old house. Once, when I went home to visit, I noticed that my father had repaired the old out house. When I inquired about this, I found that he had never used the new bathroom that we had placed in the house. My father refused to use it as he could not make himself shit in the house that he lived in. On the other hand, a shirt costing seventy five dollars leaves me feeling constipated.

There are some things that really bother my wife and one is the making of the bed as soon as one gets out of it. She always gets up before I do and expects the last person out of the bed to make it up. My reaction is that since within twelve hours you are going to get back in the bed, why make it up? We finally reached an

agreement concerning the making of the bed. I was supposed to make the bed every other day.

I aim to please.

She said to me a few days after we reached the agreement "I will do it because all you are doing is pulling the covers over the mess."

She offered to show me how to make the bed properly, but I declined.

When my wife returned from a week of visiting our daughter in Texas, she found that the bed in our bedroom was made with inordinate care.

I aim to please.

She said, "I will bet anything that you made that bed while I was on the plane from Texas."

Believe it or not, she was almost right. I only made the bed twenty minutes before picking her up from the airport.

I still aim to please.

There are two places where I place my clothes when I remove them. One is the doorknob to the bedroom door and the other is a chair that sits in a corner of our bedroom. I really don't know what I would do if they were not there. My wife hangs her clothes in her closet as soon as she removes them or places them in the hamper for clothes to be washed. When we moved into our new home, she took the walk-in closet in our bedroom and gave me the very small closet in our bedroom. I was never given a choice as to which closet in our bedroom would be mine.

When I asked her about it she said, "I have more clothes than you and you don't need it, you would just make a mess of it anyway."

My wife has more than two hundred sweaters in that closet. She has more sweaters than Imelda Marcos had shoes and she has the necessary space to keep them, since she claimed the very large closet in our bedroom.

One thing that I don't understand is the necessity of women to over buy certain items, like shoes, sweaters, dresses and underwear. Buying her a Christmas gift is like looking for a needle in a haystack. She has three of everything, I just go out and buy her some stupid item. For her fifty-first Christmas, I purchased her a doll.

The note on her Christmas gift read, "Don't let anyone tell you that I can't give you a baby."

For no reason what so ever, some years ago my wife changed the drawer where I kept my socks and now she still laughs when

I go in the previous drawer looking for them. I am a creature of habit. There are times when I come home from playing golf and find all the furniture in the house re-arranged for no good reason.

I complain but, she says, "Get used to it."

Her reason for the change was that the house was getting boring.

Like many men, I happen to like a boring house, a house where everything always stays the same. When a chair or sofa has been in the same spot for years why move it to the other side of the room. Women rearrange the furniture in their houses just to confuse their husbands. I have often suspected that rearranging the furniture coincides with a disagreement with one's mate. I really suspect that it is one way to get back at one's husband and to show him who is the real boss in the castle.

My wife uses a bathroom towel once, maybe twice at most.

My wife claims that I would use a towel until it stands up when I put it on the floor.

She said to me. "I changed your bathroom towel because it smelled up the entire bathroom."

I said to her, "It is just used for drying clean water off the body."

My wife always changes my bath towel even when it is not necessary.

She claims it smells, but it does not.

In order to survive in this house living with my wife I built a pottery shop just off the dining room. It is a place to hide. Some of my male friends ask if they can hide there from their wives, but I have turned them down.

That is my special hiding place. It stays dirty with clay, papers and tools all over the floor so my wife refuses to enter it. That is just fine with me, I like it that way. The only problem is that sometimes I can't find my pottery tools or anything else that I need in the shop. However, I can live with that. If my wife can't find something that she knows she has, it would drive her crazy.

Shortly after we moved into our new house, my wife purchased a new bed. Not that we needed one and not just any bed, I swear it is twenty feet across and takes up the entire bedroom.

I said to her once "we are in different oceans, I am in the Atlantic and you are in the Pacific."

Her comment was, "I need my space and I don't need anyone poking me."

It seems that these days everything is about space. The kitchen is her space and my space is the pottery shop. Her office is her space and my space is my office. I really think she is considering putting a lock on her office door. She has a sign on her office door that reads, "Wife's Office." The rule is that when one shares a house with another person, if that person is a husband or wife nothing seems to be more important than one's space.

My wife is constantly saying, "I need more space." Is this some kind of hint?

In our home we both have an office, complete with desks, computers, Xerox copiers and all the other necessary office equipment. There is one major difference in our offices. Her office is in perfect order. Everything in her office is in its correct place. Her office is more orderly than the halls of heaven. She has a special place for all of her office supplies. Her desk has special dividers where everything is placed just where she wants it.

Even the closet in her office has everything labeled and placed in perfect order. My office, by my own admission, is a pig sty. I can't find a damn thing in my office. My desk, unlike my wife's desk is a cluttered mess, with papers and unfinished work all over it. Now here is the rub. When I need tape, pens, scissors, staplers, correction fluid, stamps, glue or any other office supplies, I know where to find them - in her office.

What am I to do since there is nothing in my office that I can find? Even if I purchased supplies, I would not be able to find them in that jungle. I always try to replace the things that I borrow from her office.

I aim to please.

Sometimes I forget to put the items that I took from her office back where I found them. That small oversight creates a real disaster. You would think that it was the end of the world. When I think about it, I realize that no one's desk and files should be a neat as she keeps hers. It is against the Law of Entropy, which governs our universe.

Be it resolved that one should never try to explain to one's wife the nature of a scientific principle, just as one should never try to teach a wife how to drive a car, that also is a no no. I tried once to explain a basic principle of the universe to her; she wanted no part of it. I got the distinct impression that she did not believe me. I tried to explain to her that I am more in tune with nature, and the universe at large, than she is. I tried to explain that the universe seeks randomness or disorder. The universe favors those reactions which lead to a greater degree of disorder. That one of the underlying principles in Universal Physics is that the entropy {degree of disorder or randomness} of the universe strives for a maximum. My being disordered and unorganized is just a part or the master plan of the universe. I even tried to explain to her that water should really freeze at any temperature because the freezing of water is exothermic and most exothermic reactions lead to a greater degree of disorder and tend to occur spontaneously.

I said to her, "Water does not freeze at any temperature because the water molecules in the solid state are an ordered system. Water in the solid state represents an organized system which nature abhors. The freezing of water is related to the temperature and the change in entropy {randomness or disorder} and because nature wants disorder and since ice is an ordered system, very low temperatures are required for water to freeze."

I tried to explain to her that the only reason why we can't marry close kin is because nature wants randomness or disorder in the gene pool.

I said to her, "That is the reason that incest is so hideous."

If there is not sufficient randomness or disorder in the gene pool, abnormalities result in the offspring."

She didn't get it or believe me. In spite of her disbelief, I am still convinced that I am more in tune with the universe than she is because my world is one of total disorder.

My wife refuses to drive my car because she thinks it is dirty, which it is. She takes her car through a car wash station. I let mother nature wash mine every time it rains. A car is not going to last any longer if it is washed or not washed. When you trade it in the used car salesperson has already made a decision that he is not going to give you anything for it, so why wash it. There are some things on the floor and the seats of my car but there is enough room for her to sit down without complaining, anyway we seldom drive each other's car.

There is another unique thing about my wife. She has a photographic memory when it comes to where things are in the house. She can walk in a room and see my watch on the dresser and it registers something in her brain. She will see my shoes in the garage and remember that they are there. I take my class

ring off when I am making pottery and a few days later I am looking for it.

All I have to do is ask my wife where it is and with that unique brain of hers, she says, "Look in the flower room by the second pot of plants."

How she does this is beyond me, but she knows where every thing in every room of the house is located. Since I can't keep up with anything, I am always asking her where something is. True to form she always knows where whatever I am looking for is located. She claims that I spend too much of my life looking for things, by her estimate ninety percent of my life is spent looking for something, and she is probably right. She also says that I suffer from CRS {Can't remember shit}.

The Complete Book of Fussing and Nagging

My daughter, Barbra, who is a carbon copy of my wife, purchased an electronic finder for my Christmas gift. The gadget works like this; there is a master box with numbers on it and smaller boxes also with numbers. What one does is program the larger box to locate any lost item. After programming the master box it will send a signal to the smaller box and a ringing sound will tell you where the item is located.

The problem is that it does not work in reverse. After a few weeks I could not find the master box and could not locate my lost items.

It seems to me that any competent engineer would have designed the box to work both ways. Engineers just don't seem to understand how some one living in a disordered universe needs a gadget that could locate both ways. Now I am in need of an item to help me locate the locater. I guess I will ask my wife if she knows where it is, I'm sure she does.

Eating dinner is also an adventure. The first thing that my wife does is throwing all of my junk on the dinner table into my office and then starts to fuss about it.

"Every time we come to the dinner table, I have to remove your junk to make space for the meal."

I just smile and say, "I'm sorry."

I aim to please.

Her reply is always, "You sure are sorry, you are a sorry soul."

If I start to taste the food before she sits down, it is a real disaster in the making and is sure to cause her to make one of her caustic remarks.

"Are you that hungry, you can't wait for me to sit down? I am the one preparing the food or did you forget?"

I just say, "I'm sorry, you know that I love you." Her reply always is, "You only love yourself or you really are a sorry person."

Some time ago I started giving her a paper napkin at each meal. I would fold the napkin into a very, very small triangle and place it beside her plate.

She complained about this a few times saying, "Why do you do that? I just have to unfold it to use it, you jerk."

After a while she stopped commenting about it. Since it doesn't seem to annoy her any more, I guess I will just stop doing it.

I aim to please.

On a visit with her sisters {she has three} to Washington, District of Columbia, they were apparently discussing their husbands and their short comings. I think the entire trip was arranged so that they could decide which husband had the most faults. I think I got the trophy for first place.

Her sister Judy told her that her husband Mel spends seventy five percent of his life looking for things.

My wife answered, "That is an improvement over my husband by fifteen percent because he spends ninety percent of his life looking for things and five percent asking me where something is located."

It is comforting to know that I am not the only husband in the entire world that can't keep up with his possessions. There must be tens of thousands of husbands out there like that.

I think we men should form a club and call it, "Where Is My."

We both play golf or play at golf. I must admit that the golf game that I play in no way resembles the golf tournaments or golf players seen on television. Yet, golf is a serious matter in our household, for me anyway. I am competitive and I like to win. My wife doesn't care if she wins or loses. She considers it a game, I consider it more than a game. It is the ultimate experience that one can encounter in all the games of the world. Golf is more important than any other of life's games. I enjoy being able to hit the ball for distance. My wife is happy if her ball is in the fairway. When she gets to a water hole she takes out an old ball.

I try to tell her, "If you hit one of your new balls you might get over the water."

She says, "I am not going to lose one of my good golf balls."

When my ball lands in the water she says, "One new ball for the golf gods and one stupid man for the game."

She thinks that all men lose their brains when they start a game of golf. She might be right. I would rather win a two dollar bet in golf than a thousand in the lottery.

There is a joke that describes how most men feel about golf:

A foursome was on the tenth tee near a roadway. They were just getting ready to tee off. They spotted a hearse passing with many cars trailing behind it. The golfer on the tee took off his hat,

placed it over his heart and bowed his head until the hearse passed.

One of the players spoke up and asked, "What in the hell was that all about?"

The golfer put his tee in the ground and just before he hit his 300 yard drive, he said, "She was a good wife."

Many men have died on the golf course and I can't think of a better way to go.

 word of advice to those men who want to go grocery shopping with their wives. Grocery shopping is a woman's domain and men should stay away from it. It is a sure way to start a disagreement.

The last time I went grocery shopping with my wife it ended in a disaster.

I ask her a reasonable question concerning her shopping, "Do you have a shopping list?"

She said, "I have a shopping list in my head."

We then proceeded to go from isle to isle while she uses her imaginary shopping list.

I said to her, "You shop like you type, using the Columbus system, find a key and land on it, now you are finding something and buying it."

She said, "You go sit in the car and stop following me around, meddling and commenting on what I am doing, that is unless you want to pay for the food."

"I am paying for this and not you, so I will do it my way."

I left the store and went out and sat in the car, turned on the radio

and enjoyed the rest of the shopping adventure. That was better than the option of paying for the food.

I decided that it would be the last time that I would shop for groceries with her.

I aim to please.

There was one other adventure that I had concerning grocery shopping.

My wife said, "If you are going out, would you stop at the grocery store and buy some milk, we are completely out of it and I don't plan to go out."

I said, "Sure, I will stop at Food Lion and get it."

I aim to please my wife.

I came back home with the milk and put it in the refrigerator.

In the morning when she started to prepare her cereal,

she said to me, "Look at the milk that you purchased, it is butter milk."

"You went to the store and purchased the cheapest milk that you

could find, you cheap jerk and that is buttermilk. Do you expect me to use buttermilk on my cereal?"

I was at a loss for words, like any husband, I aim to please.

I had done my best to purchase what she had asked for. She should have been grateful that I even remembered to stop at the store for milk in the first place.

When you go to Food Loin to purchase milk, take a good look at the shelf. There must be fifty different types of milk, all on the same shelf, and they all read milk. There are quarts, pints, gallons, 2% milk, skim milk, 1% milk, lactose free milk, reduced fat milk, butter milk, sealtest milk, whole milk and many more all in different color containers and all marked milk. How was I to know which one to purchase? She was right, I looked at the price and

purchased the cheapest one that I could find, after all, I was paying for it. The only good thing that came out of that adventure

was that she has never again asked me to purchase milk or buy something at the grocery store when I go out and I don't understand why because I think I might've gotten it right the next time.

I aim to please.

One final thing before I turn you over to my wife. My wife and I were at the hospital visiting a sick friend. While getting on the elevator, I accidentally {on purpose} touched her butt and she turned and hit me. There was a lady, about my wife's age, that I did not see, getting on the same elevator.

The lady turned to my wife and said, "Honey, I have one at home just like him."

Shaking her fist in the air she said, "Sometimes I have to cold cock him to get him to understand."

I write this for all the men out there who have wives that fuss and nag. You should consider it in the genes of the species that we call woman. You should just sit back and enjoy it. It is harmless and I suspect that it relieves tension. It appears that all women

possess this talent and will always use it. It is a part of the cycle of life. Something the men of the Homo Sapiens species are expected to enjoy or at the very least tolerate.

BEN A. WATFORD

My Wife Fussing and Nagging

On Golf

> Impotent Pieces of the Game He plays
> Upon this Chequer - board of Nights and Days;
> Hither and thither moves, and checks, and slays,
> And one by one back in the Closet lays.
>
> *Rubiayat of Omar Khayyam*

OK, play it like a man and go for it fool! Just another new golf ball for the gold gods.

Go out and clean the golf cart, I have to play tomorrow and the cart is a mess like everything else that we own. What does "Q" in Q School stand for? It stands for the fact that you should quit wishing for the impossible.

Your swing is good? What do you want me to do, lie to you?

Yes, it is a nice day for golf or sex, so you had better take a sweater. No, take a sweater and a coat.

You will never be able to shoot your age. No one lives to be one hundred fifty, so you can forget that.

It is always what you want to do, go play golf by yourself, just stop bugging me about playing. I will play when I want to play.

So your playing partner said, "Our wives think we are having fun."

If you guys regarded it as just a game and not the end of the world, you just might enjoy playing it and have some fun. Just consider it a nice walk in the woods. Your best playing days were fifty years ago.

No, I don't want to go to the driving range. You go to the driving range. My shoulder is not well and you know it, yet you ask me to go to the driving range with you, see that is how much you love me.

Give me a break; you could not afford five minutes of Butch Harmon's golf time. Anyway he only takes people with talent and a chance to win and you don't fall in those categories.

You might have used your putter. You were only fifteen or so feet of the green, but you guys never do that because it is not the manly thing to do.

You guys have such egos. You would never use your putter off the green. I watched someone playing with Tiger Woods today and he hit his ball with his putter about fifteen feet off the green and it was up hill.

The stupid announcer said, "That is not the way one should play that shot."

The man came within two feet of the cup and he used his putter. You guys think that is not manly, all of you are full of crap. I will use my putter fifty feet off the green. I usually get closer than you with your manly way of doing things. I know that you are a man and you don't have to prove it.

I said, "Good golf shot," but that was not enough. You have to be told over and over again. Pat your own back.

I know we are playing in a tournament tomorrow morning, and that does not make me happy. I will have to play with you and you always get upset about your lousy game.

You don't have to say let's win, I am going out there to have some fun, winning is the last thing on my mind. If that is on your agenda, go play by yourself.

When you get to hell the first thing that you are going to ask Satan is, "Where is the first tee?"

When you get to hell please don't use your good balls on the holes that are surrounded by fire, they cost too much.

Instead of saying you are going to play this water hole like a man, you should say, I am going to play this hole as if I am stupid.

This is the British Open tournament and that player just wiped his golf club on his pants leg. What is wrong with you men? You do the same thing. It there something wrong with using a towel? That is what golf towels are for, they are used to clean your golf clubs. Men, including you, should not use their pants legs to clean their clubs, it is wrong. Men do it because they do not have to clean up the mess. It would be different if men had to clean their clothes. Then they would not do it.

You never see women golfers wipe their golf clubs on their clothes and you never see women golfers wipe their ball on their gloves, I don't understand why you men do it. It is because men are dirty.

You and your golf game really need to be put away forever.

You can go out and play golf by yourself or find someone else to play with. I don't want to play with someone who gets upset when he makes a bad shot, which is every time he swings.

I don't go to the golf course just to see how far I can hit the damn ball. With you, it is always, "I hit that ball two hundred and fifty yards, did you see that." Give me a break."

Why can't you just enjoy the game, you are not Tiger Woods and you never will be, so just play your lousy game and enjoy it.

We have an 8:00 o'clock tee time in the morning and you should go to bed early. The only reason that I want you to go to bed early is to get some rest, nothing else.

Golf tomorrow is the only reason I want you to go to bed early, If you have something else in mind you can stay up until the cows come home.

Your swing is really fast with all that grunting, you are trying to kill the damn ball and it will die.

You worry too much about your golf score; it is just a damn game. Try to enjoy it, if you know how.

Try cleaning the golf cart sometime.

Why can't you play with old golf balls old men try to play with old balls all the time?

Yes you can go to "Q" school, "Quit school."

You burned the seat cover on the golf cart with that stupid pipe. We can never have anything nice that you do not ruin. Nothing is sacred to you.

You know everything, so you know what is wrong with Tiger Wood's golf game. It is not that girl, as you have stated. She has been with him for more than two years. I don't care what happened to Samson in the bible. That has nothing to do with it.

Samson in the bible is just a story and has nothing to do with Tiger woods and his girl friend.

Wait a minute; all that I said was that Tiger Woods was probably getting married and that he told the reporters that he was going deep-sea fishing. You are the one who took it to mean something else.

You live unceremoniously through Tiger Woods; he plays well, like you would like to do. He also has a young blond wife with blue eyes.

So what you are asking is if the three of us were the same age, Tiger Woods, you and me, who would I marry, you guess?

Golf is just a damn game and I am not going to get upset about how I play it.

Men and golf, all you guys think about is how far you can drive the ball.

I started to buy you some Nike golf balls; they cost forty dollars a dozen. Then I remember that you would use then on water holes so I didn't buy them. I don't feel like donating forty dollars worth of golf balls to the golf gods.

All you think about is how far you can hit the golf ball, it is not how far you hit the ball it is what you do after you hit the ball and what you do is curse and throw your clubs.

Forget it; I am not talking about golf and not how long something is, can't you keep you mind out of your pants.

Does how far you hit the ball mean that you can score low, forget it?

Of course it is my fault that the golf cart cover is on wrong. You use the golf cart more than I do.

Do I want to play nine holes of golf with you? Think, I have to bowl tomorrow and I play twilight golf after that, do I look like I am twenty years old?

Golf is a game that one should enjoy playing and not get mad about a bad shot.

All you men talk about is what ball I use when playing golf, "I use a top flite", "I use an ultra", "and I use a titelist."

All the balls are the same, just like those old balls of yours.

No! I will not use my good ball to hit over the water. I don't care what you say. I don't intend to lose my good golf ball. I am going to hit an x-out, one that I found. You can hit any ball that you want too. Go on and lose one of your new golf balls.

I got the feeling that you were competing with me today; it was the way you went up and replaced my ball after Jean's ball hit it on the green. You did not put it in the right place; you placed it further back than it should have been.

I really don't understand why you old men can't go out and enjoy a round of golf without getting upset with your lousy play.

You guys would have fun if you realize that golf is just a game and not the end of the world. If you did not get upset with your lousy play and just consider it a nice walk in the woods. You should be happy that a bunch of old men can still walk. You guys are obsessed with how far you can hit the stupid ball and how many pars you don't get. You will never enjoy the game with your attitude.

Sometimes I think you are in a different world from me. It is just a game, golf is just a game, and it is not the beginning and end of all things.

Why are you so competitive, you should just enjoy your game and not worry so much about winning?

No, I told you before that I don't want to go out and play nine holes. Go by yourself or find some of your friends to play with. If you were not so grumpy you would be able to find someone to play with and would not always asking me.

Why get upset over a damn game, learn to have fun when you play. I don't know why I say that or expect you to take my advice, you are the way that you are and nothing is going to change that.

Throw your clubs, get upset with your lousy play, donate golf balls to the golf gods and see who gives a damn.

You can't get down like that to see your golf shot because you do not have fifteen year old legs like she does. Just forget it and putt the damn ball.

Sure I used to play lots of golf. "Used to" died and is gone forever."

This is the last time that I am going to ask you, stop wiping your golf clubs on your pants, it's disgusting.

Did you ask me how I felt when you came in from playing golf? No!

The first thing that came out of your mouth was "I'm hungry."

You never do anything right. I noticed when we were playing golf the other day that you have to put your ball at least three inches in front of the markers when you drive your golf ball. That is against all of the rules of golf that I have ever read.

When we lift and place in inclement weather you always place your ball closer to the green. Don't you realize that is dishonest? I have noticed that all you old men do that and the ladies never place their ball closer to the green in the lift and place mode.

I move my ball back and you move your ball forward, that is wrong and you know it.

Women never do that when they play golf they play by the rules of the game.

What difference does it make with what ball you play with? No one plays with your old balls but you anyway.

You don't change your agenda no matter what. Your daughter and her children are coming and you are going to play golf.

Is golf more important than your daughter? You don't have to answer that, I know the answer.

I don't like the crystal golf balls and I will not play with them. There are some other balls that I don't want to play with either.

What do you mean, you need that putt, we are a four-person team and you are not playing alone, the team needs the putt. You always say that.

When you play golf why do you have to say, that is my fault? It is no one's fault, we win as a team or we lose as a team.

I am just asking a question about the damn game, never mind, I don't feel like talking to you.

You have absolutely no conversational skills, none at all. I don't know why I even try to talk to you.

When we are on the golf course and you talk, all that you say is, "Watch my drive" or "look how close my ball is the pin or I made a great putt."

Who gives a damn but you?

No, I am not going to play tomorrow and I don't have to tell you why I am not playing. You can play by yourself or you can call some of your friends, if you have any. If I don't play what are you going to do about it? As if I care.

"Yes, you could play in the PGA, Poor Golfers Association."

You complain about your back hurting and then go out and play, you are a dumb man, you really are. So just go on out with your hurting back.

No, I am not interested in playing nine holes of golf, forget it, and that is the only hole that you are going to play with.

Yes, we have the tickets. I know that we are going to the Augusta National Tournament and you think you deserve a green jacket. If you want a green jacket you had better stop at Wal-Mart on the way there, because that is the only way that you are going to get a green jacket.

No way! I don't want to play golf; you are crazy, playing golf in this weather. It is ninety seven degrees out there.

You don't need sports psychologist for your game, what you need is pair of eyeglasses, hearing aid and a cane.

There was very little in the shop to purchase with our chits. That is why I spent so much money on a gift for you that you are not going to want but you are going to get it anyway.

You are going to try "Q" school. I am laughing because you have some strange goals. "Q" school is for good golfers and not hackers.

You can barely break one hundred on the golf course and you are talking about "Q" school. They don't let people in "Q" school with handicaps above twenty-two.

It is not fun to play with someone who gets upset when he makes a bad shot and makes many of them. It is just a damn game.

You are not a golfer you are a hacker. Golfers shoot low scores not high ones, and ninety seven is a high score.

There are lots of things in life that are more important than a game of golf. No not that, that and golf are all that is in that small brain of yours.

Why should I play with you, so that I can watch you hit the ball and comment: "Watch how far I hit the ball?" Watch that flag stick and see how close I come?

Forget it, I would rather play with the ladies.

I play nine holes in the twilight with you and that is enough. Why should I punish myself by playing with someone who just wants to win and get upset when he hits a bad shot or puts his new ball in the lake?

I don't care who beats me at as long as they count right.

It is just a game, what does it matter if you win or lose a game of golf? You don't make a living playing golf. Hackers don't make money from the game of golf.

Men lose their brains when they start playing a game of golf.

I still say, men, golf and brains are not a perfect mix and not the right equation for playing a round of golf.

Now you are upset because your new ball belongs to the golf gods, why don't you use an old ball or a special water ball when you try to hit over water.

No! You have to play the hole like a man and go for it, well you did and now your new ball is gone.

I still have my new ball and where is yours, in the damn lake.

You have two old balls in your pants, so don't worry about it.

The cart is a mess like your desk. Look at other people's golf carts and see if theirs are filled with junk.

I am ashamed to use the cart, the other women will not want to ride with me. Go out and clean the mess that you have made of the cart.

Did you plug the cart in after you used it? No, you did not.

I will not hit my good ball over the water, you can do it if you want to but it is a dumb move.

Your ball is now at the bottom of the lake, and I still have my new ball and no penalty stroke, Mr. Smarty.

It is just a game so if I win or lose I don't care, I am out here to enjoy myself.

I don't feel like playing today or tomorrow or the next day. Go play by your self.

All you can think about is how far you drive the ball. I don't want to hear about it.

What does it matter how far you drive the damn ball? It's the accuracy that counts. not how far you drive. Like a lot of things it's not the length that counts.

Your golf game is always about you and how you play, get a life.

Have you backed the cart out and put my clubs on it. No! You stand around here and wait for me to do it.

I don't feel like playing, get some of your friends to play. No, I am not your friend so forget it. I am not a wife so you can forget that too.

No, I don't want to go with you; you are just going to the club house to register for Saturday, go by yourself.

You are really a piece of work. a know-it-all and a general pain in the neck. Get a life and get some friends and stop asking me to do things with you. Play by yourself or call some of your friends to play with you and leave me alone. I enjoy being by myself without you picking on me. I need my own space and time alone.

No! I don't want to play three holes of golf with you because you can't count. If I go with you, will you not stop at the third hole?

No! I don't want to play one hole of golf with you because you don't know what one hole is. If I go with you, you will not stop until you have played nine or eighteen holes. So just go by yourself and forget it.

You leave for the golf outing on Wednesday, {CRS again} can't remember shit.

I like the way that we come in from playing golf and you prepare your dinner. Did you ask if I wanted mine prepared? All that you think about is number one.

I just can't believe it, he came in here and fixed his dinner and never even asked me if I wanted something to eat.

You are pathetic, the way you walk the way you talk, the way you play golf, you are a pathetic man.

Do whatever you enjoy doing as long as it does not include me, so forget it.

I said I would play three holes of golf with you yesterday and it turned into nine holes, so forget it.

I am not playing today so get out of here.

What you need is a new body and ten thousand golf lessons.

I can understand how football players and baseball players leave college to play their sport. Their useful years are limited but golf players can play at golf forever, old and bent over men, like you, can go on trying to play forever.

No, I don't think that they are going to pick you as Captain of the American Ryder Cup team. They don't pick old men and especially old Black men.

Did you talk with the fellows that you played with today, then why do you have to talk to me with your silly shit? Go into your shop and play with your clay.

At least you were out playing today, think of how many people who wish they could have been playing golf. There a lot who are pushing up daisies so stop your complaining about how poorly you played. You always play poorly.

Look at your pants, you wiped your clubs or your hands on your pants, not only do you do it, but I see the professionals do it. If you guys had any common sense or had to clean your pants you would be more careful and not do something dumb like that.

You guys even wipe your clubs on your pants' legs, you will not see the ladies ever do something like that. Women are smarter than men and like things clean and neat.

Look at that damn golfer he's wiping his club on his pants just like someone else that I know. Golfers should carry a towel to wipe their clubs, ball and their dirty hands on.

Yes, you play like Tiger Woods, you both play with golf clubs.

No! You do not look like a golfer, you look like John Daly, only he is a bit more erect.

With that look on Tiger's face, he is not going to do well. I have seen that look on your face many times and you never play golf well.

Go on and hit your new ball over the water, you will never make it and you are just donating a good golf ball to the golf gods.

No, I am not going to use a new ball; I am going to use one of my water balls. It is a ball that I found the other day and it is as old as dirt and I don't mind losing it or donating it to the golf gods. Anyway I am not going to hit my golf ball towards the water; I have enough sense to go around it.

When the ladies make a good shot or make a nice putt they hug each other. When you men make a good shot or nice putt you have to hit each other and that seems stupid to me.

You are right, I would hug my caddie, especially if he looked like Alex Trebeck, hug the hell out of him.

Why get upset with how lousy you play golf. You are not a great golfer so just forget it and consider it a nice day out of the house.

I enjoy golf because it is fun and I don't have to make a living doing it. You play golf to get angry with yourself when you make a bad shot, which is often. When are you going to learn to enjoy the game and not get upset about how you play? You are a lousy golfer so live with that knowledge.

I will play golf with you if you promise not to get upset about how you play, use an old ball when we get to the water hole and promise to play only nine holes.

You had three dozen crystal balls, what happened to them? I know the golf gods that guards the water holes has them.

You went to Maryland to play golf with your buddies for two days and had to rush back after the second day. It is the same way when we go anyplace, you are always in a hurry to get back home. If that is the reason you rushed back you can just go again.

I expected to have at least three days to myself. I need some time just to have a quiet and peaceful house, no alcohol, no looking for things and not having to fix meals.

You must have had lousy golf games to come back so quickly. What did you expect, to shoot your age, you are not one hundred fifty yet, but you are getting there.

Water balls? I know what you do with water balls, you put them in the water for the golf gods.

When are you going to learn the limits of your ability, you old man.

One day you are going to learn that golf is just a game. It is a game that one should enjoy and not curse and get upset over.

You should not throw your clubs. The clubs did not cause the poor shot, you did.

You will learn that one day after I put your ashes in the sand trap by the eighteenth green.

I purchased you those Nike golf balls as a Christmas present. I don't expect you to hit them like Tiger Woods and I surely don't want you to use them when you come to a water hole. Try to remember that those golf balls are for you and not the golf gods, who hang around holes surrounded by water.

You used the new Nike golf balls; I hope you did not use them on water holes because they cost four dollars each.

I think that it is all in your head, there isn't a dimes worth of difference in all the golf balls on the market.

The major difference in golf balls on the market is the price and you men have never learned that.

You would try any gimmick that comes along and says that it will reduce you score.

They sell a lot of x-out golf balls, so other people use them besides me. That was a really dumb statement.

Give it time and you will shoot your age, if you live to be one hundred fifty.

You can go and play golf if you want too. I am not going to play today because I just don't want to. I play when I feel like playing.

There is more to life than golf, I don't mean that, you know what I mean.

That is why your game is so lousy, you always have your little mind on something unimportant.

It might be important to you but it is not important to me.

You are on the golf course playing golf, while the woman does everything around the house. I am the woman, for your information, thanks for asking.

You guys sit around and expect the woman of the house to do everything. You are retired, you make your pots. play golf or poker or whatever else you do. Yet, you expect me to do everything, buy this, call that person, fix this and find that. You should have stayed in that dumb town that you grew up in and married some stupid woman that would follow your orders. Learn to do things yourself and stop asking me to do them.

The Bathroom

With them the seed of Wisdom did I sow,
And with my own had wrought to make it grow,
And this was all the Harvest that I reap'd.
"I came like Water, and like the Wind I go."

Rubaiyat of Omar Khayyam

Why don't you watch where you are aiming that thing of yours and stop peeing all over the bowl?

You should keep your eye on what you are doing when you pee and you would not pee all over the damn bowl and the floor.

Why can't you sit down like women do when they pee? What! You don't want to get it wet!

Forget it, stop flattering youself, it is not that long.

If you had to clean the bathroom, you would watch what you are doing.

I notice that you sit down when you have to shit, why can't you sit when you pee.

I still don't understand why you can't sit when you use the bathroom and don't give me that crap about it getting wet.

It is only long when you are in the bed and poking me or when you get up in the morning.

You were lost and refused to ask for direction. I will never understand why men can't ask for direction when they are totally lost.

It's that same man macho thing that makes you guys have to stand and pee all over the place. It might be different if you watched what you were doing when you pee or drive.

The bathroom is not a fire hydrant and the floor in the bathroom is not a stream.

Come in here I want to show you what to do with the lid on the bathroom stool. See I put it up, now that I am finished I will close it. Do you understand?

You put the toilet paper in the rack and you put it in backwards.

That is not the way that one puts toilet paper in the rack.

Where are you going with that book, the bathroom is not a library.

If you want to read, go in the study, just in case someone else wants to use the bathroom.

I know there are other bathrooms in this house but that is the one in our bedroom that I always use.

What are you doing "old man" peeing in Morse code, dot dot dash, dot dot dash?

I will be off the stool in a minute or can an old man wait that long?

You should live with another man so that the two of you could live in a pigsty.

Why do you have to turn on the light to pee? Oh well, I guess you had better do it, otherwise you will pee all over the damn seat.

Is the lid on the toilet seat too heavy for you to lift, if so, call me and I will lift it for you.

You are going to the bathroom; I hope that you sit down in there.

I notice that you got a towel out of the bathroom cabinet to use in your shop.

How did I know that you got a towel, as usual you did not close the cabinet drawer.

Did you lift the lid on the toilet seat before you peed, I don't think so?

It was not water from washing you hands, unless you used yellow water to wash your hands.

How many times would you use that towel? If you place it on the floor, it would stand. There are plenty of towels on the shelf for you use.

I don't think you would ever change bath towels if I didn't do it.

I changed your bathroom towel because it smelled up the entire bathroom.

If I have told you once I have told you a thousand times, hold your head down when you brush your teeth and you will not make a mess of the mirror.

Is that so very, very hard to do?

You have an electric toothbrush, learn how to use it. Just don't look in the mirror when you clean your teeth.

You don't have to look in the mirror to see what you are doing, it is not necessary to look in the mirror when you brush your teeth. Come with me in the bathroom and watch me brush my teeth and see if I make a mess of the mirror or the bowl.

You make a mess all over the counter.

Don't you realize that? If you had to clean up that mess, you would be more careful.

When you brush your teeth learn to lean over the sink and not get that mess all over the place.

Why do you feel that you have to look in the mirror when you brush your teeth? Does it make your teeth cleaner?

You make a mess all over the counter. Don't you realize that?

If you had to clean up that mess, you would be more careful.

Don't you know how to brush your hair with your hand? Try it you might like it.

Why do you have to open a new bar of soap every time you use the bathroom?

Can't you see the soap or is it that you don't want to use a small piece of soap.

I am going to roll up the towels that you left unrolled. Why do you have to be so messy?

I get sick of picking up after you.

Why can't you watch what you are doing when you pee? You are still looking up at the ceiling, out the window and all around the room and you don't pee straight.

You get pee all over the commode and the floor.

Who do you think cleans up the mess you make in the bathroom?

The cleaning lady has to clean up your mess. I don't care if you do pay her to do it, it is not right.

Did you leave the water on in the bathroom? It was running full force; you have to be more careful.

I still don't understand why men can't sit on the commode and pee like women do.

Yes, you could sit on the stool and pee!

Just forget it, that is a stupid thing to say and you have said it before. You don't have to worry about getting it wet.

If you had to clean the bowl, you would sit when you used it or you would be more careful.

I don't care if the house cleaner does do the cleaning, you should be more considerate.

I am going to teach you what a shower curtain is used for. Come into the bathroom with me.

See the shower curtain. It is designed to keep water off the floor of the bathroom.

When you get in the shower, you pull the shower curtain so that it covers the entire bathtub.

If that is done properly, water does not get on the bathroom floor.

Can you remember that, or is it too much trouble to close the damn shower curtain.

Ashes everywhere, coffee stains on the table and you put the crap from your pipe in the toilet stool.

You are getting picky and pokey in your old age. You don't have to say it. I know what you are thinking.

On Clothes And Dressing

Ah, with the Grape my fading Life provide,
And was my Body whence the life has died.
And in a Winding sheet of Vine leaf wrapt,
So bury me by some sweet Garden side.

Rubiayat of Omar Khayyam

Where did you find that shirt, you have on blue, green and red and nothing matches? You are hopeless. No one dresses like that.

Go look in the mirror, you have on a blue shirt, green pants and red socks. That is not the way you should be dressed if you are going with me.

You really are a slob and you are not going to dinner with me dressed like a rainbow. Go to the bedroom and I will pick out something for you to wear.

What would you do with your clothes if the chair and the doorknob were not in the bedroom?

The chair and the doorknob are not made for your dirty clothes, try the clothes hamper.

Do you know what clothes hangers are for, I don't think so.

I hope that when you die and go down below you will find a chair and a doorknob.

Otherwise you will have no place for your clothes.

You have no sense of adventure. You wear the same

clothes for days and they never match.

You put on your clean clothes to go out and play golf and then go in that dirty shop and work and now you will go out with clay on yourself.

You are weird, you wear those stupid clothes to go to the store and yet you don't like the trash container in the study because it has a plastic bag in it.

So you go out and buy a trash container with a lid. That is a sheer waste of money. Just because the other one didn't look good to you. You have some weird spending

habits.

Why are you wearing short pants this time of the year?

What are you trying to do, show those bandy legs?

Go in and change clothes, don't go anyplace like that.

When you go out the way you dress is a reflection upon me.

That brown shirt does not match your blue pants; there are some colors that just don't go together.

You should realize that some colors just don't go together, unless you are a clown?

Yes, you are a fashionable dresser but you have your own fashion.

There you go getting one of your best shirts to go and work in the shop. Why not put on an old shirt? One that you would not wear anywhere, I know you would wear anything anywhere.

There are three sweaters already on that chair do you have another one for it.

There you go putting on your good sweater to wear in that pottery shop.

I don't understand how you treat the clothes you are wearing, you use your good clothes to work in that pottery shop. Go get some old clothes and wear them in there. No intelligent person would destroy his best clothes by working in that dirty shop.

You have a faded pair of blue pants that you should wear and destroy in that damn shop.

No, you have to wear the best outfits that you have to get dirty in that dirty shop of yours.

Do you do these things just to give me something to nag and fuss about?

When was the last time that suit of yours was in the cleaners, unbelievable.

I really don't care what they charge to clean a suit, you should have it clean at least every ten years.

Are those clean pants that you are going to wear in that dirty shop?

I still haven't managed to clean the last pair of pants that you wore in the shop.

I will never understand how you can wear your good clothes to work in that dirty shop. You have no sense of value when it comes to your clothes.

Then you expect them to come clean.

You are going to change aren't you, you really look tacky.

You are going to put that coat up aren't you?

Please don't put your clothes on the floor, put them where they belong.

Why can't you put on the ones that you had on yesterday? If you are going to work in that dirty shop wear some old clothes.

You would think differently if you had to wash them.

They are not my shoes and I am not the one who should be carrying them back and forth to the shoe shop to have them fixed. You are the one who should be doing that.

You should consider buying a new pair of shoes. I know they would cost money, so what?

There you go with that sweater again. You have lots of sweaters and you always pick that one. Is there something wrong with your other sweaters?

Why do you want to wear the same thing all of the time, you have other clothes? You are not a creature of habit, you are a lousy dresser.

Are you going to change your clothes before you go in your pottery shop?

You should not work in your pottery shop with your good clothes on.

For the last time, change your clothes before you go into that damn pottery shop.

You will not get them dirty! You will get them dirty just by walking through that door.

Why are these coats on the floor, you put then on the floor? I go to look for something and the place is a mess, I swear.

That child owns all those coats and he puts on one that is ragged and dirty, good heavens.

I am different from you; I have things that I wear on special occasions and things that I wear around the house.

You will wear your best clothes just to work in that damn pottery shop. You never consider what you are putting on and you mess up your best clothes in all of that clay mess.

You put on the same pants that you had on yesterday

and they have clay on them. None of the clothes that you are wearing match, you are not going out with me with those clothes on.

I have nice clothes, so I don't have to walk around the house or go someplace looking like shit, like someone else I know.

I don't want to hear. "I'm sorry" because you don't mean it.

It's the same thing that children say and it means leave me alone about where I put my clothes.

That man owns all those coats and he puts on one that is ragged and dirty every single time, good heavens. What is so special about that dumb coat.

Your closet is full of clothes, you don't have to take them out of the basket. You wear the same coat over and over. I threw out that nasty blue shirt that you wore everyday. That shirt was faded, torn and worn out and you just kept putting it on. You can cry if you like but that shirt is gone. I just got tired of seeing you wear it every day, so I threw it out.

Why do you roll your sweater sleeves up like that, they are made to the correct length and you should not roll them up?

I can't understand why you put on your pants like that, you always put on your pants first and then your shirt.

You have to then unbutton your pants to put your shirt in, that is crazy.

Those things need washing, do you ever think of that. Don't put them back on.

Is there something wrong with your other shirts, what are you saving them for?

I am talking to you about your clothes and you are on the computer, you have not heard a word that I have said.

I buy you nice clothes and you still wear the old ones, you are a dream, a bad dream.

You would buy all of your clothes at Wal-Mart. I would not go in that store for anything.

CRS again, you purchased this sweater for me about four years ago. You did not buy it at Belks, you bought it at Wal-mart.

I know that because the one that you purchased was too large and I had to take it back and exchange it.

There you go again with one of your good sweaters going into that nasty shop. You have an old green sweater you know.

Why can't you wear an old sweater to work in that dirty place?

I am going to keep the basket that contains the clothes that I have just washed out here. There is no need for you to go in the basket for clothes. You have a closet full of clothes and you still wear the same ones day after day.

You are putting on a different pair of pants and you are putting the ones that you had on in the chair. There are five sweaters in that chair already and you are now going to add to the mess.

You wear the same thing over and over. In your closet you must have at least thirty shirts and you go in and pick the same shirt every time. You might be a creature of habit but it is a bad habit. What is wrong with your nice shirts? The one you are wearing is thin enough to see through from all the washing.

What are you saving your good shirts for, so that you can be buried in them? You only need one for your burial. I forgot, your cremation.

I wear nice clothes because I am concerned with how I look and you wear old clothes because you don't care how you look.

I don't understand your choice in clothes, you are like a hobo.

I am putting out the clothes that I am going to wear tomorrow. Yes, I am going to make sure that the colors match.

You are going to pick out your clothes also. Well, you don't have to find a sweater because there are four on the chair over there.

Where did you go to look for your coat? Did you go to where you left it or look on the rack where I placed it after you took it off and left it in the kitchen?

On Drinking

Then to this earthen Bowl did I adjourn
My lip the secret Well of Life to learn:
And lip to lip it murmur'd - "While you live,
Drink! - for once dead, you never shall return."

Rubaiyat of Omar Khayyam

*P*lease don't quote that stupid ass poem to me because you just use it as an excuse to have a drink.

"Drink, for once dead you shall never return." You are an idiot like the one who made that up. You just use that as an excuse to have a drink of wine. You don't need an excuse or a reason to drink. You will drink no matter what.

That is an alcoholic for you, denial, denial and denial.

You could teach anyone the art of denial.

I have said it once and I will say it again, anyone who drinks alcohol, no matter how much or how little they drink, is an alcoholic.

Why do you have to fill your glass so full, don't you realize that you can always go back for more?

Why don't you drink out of a paper cup like the other alcoholics?

You think that you have class because you use a glass for your drinks, people with class don't drink alcohol at all.

I have said it before and I will say it again, anyone who drinks alcohol is an alcoholic. A single drink makes you an alcoholic.

Drinking out of a wine glass doesn't give you class.

You may as well drink out of a paper cup and carry it in a paper bag like the rest of the bums.

Why do you get so uptight that you have to use outside influences, you do that all the time, a drink of alcohol?

Is this what I buy orange juice for, your vodka? I thought orange juice was for breakfast. Just try to remember that with your CRS.

I buy more orange juice than food and it just disappears along with your vodka.

I know that you had a drink because you did not put the orange juice back where it belongs.

I can never keep orange juice for breakfast; you use it in that gin or whatever you drink each night. When are you going to buy your own orange juice?

You can get a glass of wine but you can't get or find anything else.

If beer affects a baby inside a mother, it is bad for you also.

Are you going to sit there and tell me that beer does not harm an old man like you?

I don't think what you are doing is funny, bringing up crap like that. I don't know where you get your stupid knowledge. Alcohol is good for the body, sure it is good for the body, and it preserves the body after death.

There was not much in the wine glass when you knocked it over. You are using that excuse to get another glass of wine.

I consider it an insult when you offer me alcohol, yet you will keep on doing it.

People who drink alcohol have a problem and you have many problems.

You and your sister Abbie were really brother and sister. The two of you sat around drinking alcohol all the time, a bunch of drunks.

Try not having a drink at night and see if you can sleep better. I am not going to do that, so have your drink.

If I lived here alone, there would no alcohol in this house. I don't use alcohol and there would be none around here.

In my house I don't want, beer, wine or any other alcoholic drink. I would never use that poison.

Give me the phone and I will hold it while you get your poison.

Pour your own wine. I don't pour wine for anyone and I don't drink wine.

Anyone who has a drink each night is a drunk, and you have a glass of wine or other stupid drink each night.

Now you are blaming the food for your weight and not the alcohol that you drink.

Weight doesn't matter; you have to have that beer, don't you?

What do you have against drinking water; it would do you a lot more good than the alcohol that you consume.

Why don't you drink wine out of a paper cup or drink it out of the bottle like the rest of the alcoholics and bums, drinking it out of a glass does not make it right?

Drinking has nothing to do with class and it is not a male ritual. You should be able to watch a game of football on television without a beer.

You always come up with something stupid to justify your bad habits. It doesn't work with me so forget it.

Drinking out of a glass doesn't mean that you have class or that you are not a drunk.

So you are drinking white wine with my chicken, what would you have done if there had been no white wine? You would drink red, that's what!

Ugh! You have been drinking, I can smell it a mile away, stay away from me with that smell.

I hate the smell of alcohol and you know that, so just stay away from me if you have to drink that stuff.

The only difference between you and a wine "O" is that you drink your wine out of a wine glass rather than a bottle.

You drink wine everyday but you don't want the same food everyday, why not?

I don't drink alcohol because I don't need a crutch and you do.

Close the cabinet door and you could have used a paper cup for that drink.

What you want is just another glass of wine. Why don't you tell the truth?

I don't drink alcohol and I don't want to be around people who drink.

Now you put that nasty stuff on the counter.

Must you insist that I have a drink; you know very well how I feel about alcohol. Why do you do that? You do that just to be a pill and to annoy me.

What are you going to drink with your dinner? Why should I ask you that, I know what you are going to drink, wine?

I don't know why I even ask that, I know what you are going to drink, wine, like the rest of the wine O's?

You are not French and I don't give a shit how much the French drink. The French do many things that I would not think of doing. Everyone knows if the French can pronounce it or spell it they will do it.

Go get your own dinner and then you can pour your own wine. I don't drink wine and I don't pour that poison for anyone.

Fix your own damn dinner and don't complain about the food. It has nothing to do with the food that you are eating; it's all that wine you drink.

Don't touch that glass, why do you have to use that glass to drink your wine. You are just going to break it or something worse. It has to be washed by hand and you are not going to do that.

One of those new glasses was a gift to me and I don't want to see your hands on it. It is my property and I intend to keep it. I don't care what happens to it when I am gone but now it is mine and not yours.

If you only knew how much I hate alcohol, you would stop buying it and drinking it but, I don't think you are capable of caring.

I don't have any respect for people who buy alcohol or people who drink alcohol.

There you go again with that special glass for your wine. I have to wash it by hand every morning.

Why don't you get two glasses of wine at the same time. I am talking about the way that you fill the glass. Why do you have to fill it to the brim. You always spill it and I have to clean it up. There was red wine on the counter when I got up this morning. I cleaned it up for you because you were not going to do it.

No one but you is going to drink that stuff anyway, so you can just take a half glass at a time. You can't walk straight with it old man and you know that you are going to spill some of it.

Quote your stupid ass poem, see if I care;

"Then to this earthen Bowl did I adjourn
My lip the secret Well of Life to learn:
And lip to lip it murmured - "While you live,
Drink! - for once dead, you never shall return."

On Sex

But leave the Wise to wrangle, and with me
The quarrel of the Universe let be:
And, in some corner of the Hubbub couht,
Make Game of that which makes as much of thee.

Rubaiyat of Omar Khayyam

Why did you buy me flowers, thanks, but no thanks? Forget it, flowers are not enough reason to make me do that.

I know how I feel now and it is not going to change in the near future.

Please don't give me all that stuff about the flowers. I have known you for too many years and I know how you are and what you want.

I know why you brought the flowers, like everything else that you do for me.

I don't feel like getting nailed tonight so you can forget it. No buying me flowers or candy will not do the trick.

You seem to think that buying something for me involves sex and it does not.

Take a cold shower and forget it.

Maybe sometime in the next week or the next month you might get lucky. If you keep pestering me, it will be next year or the next decade.

You don't get cancer by not having sex. How can you say something that is so weird?

So the doctor said, "If you did not get sex you would die of prostate cancer."

Well you had better start on your will.

I love you too, but not that much.

I heard what you said and I am ignoring it. You get what you deserve and when you deserve it.

For the one thousandth time I will not tell you when I am going to bed. Can you get that fact threw that thick skull of yours. I do not need company when I go to bed

No, I don't want to pat your butt, anyway young men have nice tight butts and you have a wide flabby one.

You should live on your memories and leave me alone about sex.

All I said was that the battery in your watch is dead. Now you are referring to something else and that is dead also and has been dead for a long time.

I don't give a damn what the national average is once a year is too much for me.

You need something to keep you busy, then you would stop asking me stupid questions. You know that the answer is going to be no, so why do you keep asking.

There really must be something about the word "No" that confuses you. When I say no I mean no! Can't you get that through that thick head of yours?

I said no! Do you have any idea what the word means?

I would love to have a conversation with you that would not involve sex, just once.

Go away! What is this let us kiss you stuff; you are a pain in the ass.

I feel like I always feel, thank you, I am going to feel better around 2025, maybe. So you can just go back in the study because nothing is going to happen.

You say you love me, but I don't need your kind of love.

I really don't think you have an understanding of the meaning of the word love.

You never give me a chance to ask, every time I turn around your pants are unzipped.

I am not going into the bedroom, dream on fella.

In spite of what you think when a woman says no it does not mean maybe. I am not one of those women that you knew when you were growing up in that hick town.

Valentine's Day card from your wife sent by Yahoo to husband: "To husband, I miss you. Hi there, since I can't be there with you this is what I want you to do. Put your right hand behind your left shoulder. Now take your left hand and put it behind your right shoulder and squeeze. This is a perfect way for us to hug because your hands can't wander in places that I don't want them to go."

Two minutes! It would take you two minutes to find it, give me a break please.

You think your charm will get you everything, your charm hasn't worked on me in a very long time.

Ask Mary {five fingers Mary} she might be available for a good nailing tonight.

I don't care how often we *used to do it*, I told you once before, "Used to do it" died a horrible death and went straight to hell.

Anyway old men don't need love or sex.

You are not just old, you are ancient.

What you need is a cold shower and to leave me alone. I need my space.

You can go to hell and don't pass go and don't try to collect any booty.

Why do you always have to be touching and feeling? I am sitting here resting my eyes and in you come. Just go away, I need someone around that I can talk to about something other than sex.

I protect these tits because they are mine. They are on my body and not yours. Touch or feel your own damn tits.

I am going to bed now, no, you do not need to come in there with me.

You are out of your blood pressure medicine, take one of mine, it might make you impotent, no! Take two.

I am not going to bed early and if you keep that up I will not go to bed at all.

No, I am not happy because you want to see my tits; you would look at anyone's tits.

You don't have to be romantic, you don't know how. Making the bed has nothing to do with romance.

This dumb man walks around the house evil, mean and nasty and wants to know when he will get love, he means sex.

I have said it once and I will say it again. Old men don't need sex or love. What old men need is a hearing aid, wheel chair or a cane, in that order.

Sure I look good, oversized shirt and no bra, and there is the real reason, no bra.

Black men like blondes with blue eyes; they think they are in heaven when they score.

It is the same as the Massa who liked black women, men are pigs and stupid.

There is one thing that I can say about you, and that is you never give up, you may as well give up.

I am not going to feel well for the next five years, so just forget it.

Yes, I have had this headache for two months and I don't think it is ever going away.

What do I think they invented beds for? Beds were invented for people to sleep in and that is just what I intend to do.

You can't be trusted at all, so I don't want you kissing my hand.

Touch your own tits and kiss your own hand, if you need to do something stupid like that.

Most of the time you do not know how to touch, when you do you rub holes on me. No one ever taught you how to caress.

When you go to hug me you always put your head on my boobs. Just wait and I will hug you and show you how to do it properly. Just keep your hands to yourself.

Is it any of your business as to whether I am wearing a bra or not. I don't ask you if you are wearing any underwear.

Just stop looking at me; you are looking at my chest, just stop it.

It is an invasion of my privacy.

The organ that you should be thinking with is in your head not in your pants.

You did not say please and it would be no difference even if you did say please.

Who do you think you are, talking about girls; you are a bent over old grandfather.

I am going to bed and I don't want you in this bed poking me.

You don't have any feelings, you just ask me to do it just to be a pain, so forget it.

You may as well not ask because I am not going to answer and if I did the answer it would be no.

Do you really think that you are mature, I don't think so?

No mature person acts the way that you do, you have not passed your tenth birthday.

You hit a home run and then stopped at first base.

You want to know what you did wrong, what were you looking at. No! What were you looking at? You know where your eyes were and I know where they were, looking at my chest.

You base your entire existence on what you think you can do in bed and I use the term "think" loosely.

So you say that you love me and I gave you a response, that is all that you are going to get, now leave me alone.

You are too damn needy.

There is nothing in that peanut brain of yours but sex, food and wine.

Why do you ask me a question and when I answer, you deny what my answer is.

Wait a few minutes and I will put my clothes on and then I will give you a hug.

Does it make a difference if I have clothes on, yes, to you it makes a difference.

You will get your hug but you will have to wait a few minutes,

I have to get dressed.

I will hug you after I put my shirt on. All you wanted to do is feel my tits. You don't want a hug and you really have any idea what I want. I will tell you, I want my space.

"Come in here and let me hug you," and then your hands are all over me. I don't appreciate it. You are such a big jerk.

What are you looking at? There is no tick on my chest and if there is, I will take it off, thank you.

You want a hug? You can forget it.

You did not want a hug after all. What you wanted was to feel my tits.

Every time I say something to you for a little sympathy, your

Answer is to reward me with a hug, "Come let me hug you," you are getting your jollies out of it not me.

Yes, I am an old lady with big boobs that are not to be mashed on a constant basis, every time I turn around here you come grabbing and groping.

You always want to be rubbing something, rub yourself.

There is nothing in your quality time for me. You are the one who is going to be feeling better because that is your tit touching and ass grabbing time

You can hardly stand, you can hardly walk, you have pains in your shoulders, pains in your back and still all you think about is sex.

Just don't touch my tits or my arm, if you do you are going to lose a finger.

No! I don't want you around to do that, get Mary to do it.

What you call getting a piece is what has always gotten you in trouble, Mister know it all.

What do you know about what women want, you don't know anything about what women want or don't want.

All that is on that small brain of yours is sex, grow up, you are seventy four years old and you don't need it.

I don't think old men need love, sex or hugging, so get out of here and give me my space.

I am talking to you about using the phone correctly, and you think you can change the subject by bringing up some other stupid topic. I know what you are doing and I am too intelligent to accept it.

You don't need sex; you are too old to think about it. Take a cold shower because it is all in your mind.

Whatever it is that I am doing tonight; you can bet I won't be doing it with you.

I intend to get a good night's sleep without you poking me, so just move over and go to sleep.

You don't have a clue as to what I want to do; it is certainly not what you want to do.

You want something. What you want you have, you get nothing here.

I don't want to know what old men want or need; I did not marry an old man.

Keep picking at my butt and I am going to slap the shit out of you.

No! I don't want to make love with you; do you think I am looking for punishment?

I want you to read this article written by Dr. Gott. You will see that I am not the only old woman out there that does not need or want sex. Why should I do something that I don't enjoy and is punishment for me. Read it and weep because I will have this headache for the next twenty years.

No! I will not. Why should I call you when I go to bed? I don't want you dipping and doping on me.

You have a headache. What do you want me to get for you?

You can forget that.

I will have a headache for the next twenty two years, so not tonight, my love, maybe next year.

I am more than a pair of tits, yet according to you that is all that I am, two big boobs.

I know where your brains are, between your legs, that is why you have a one track mind.

Yes, you have a brain and it is in your pants. I can't believe that I married you. It is not that my mind is on sex but I know how you think and that stupid look on your face.

No! I am not interested in taking a nap with you; anyway a nap is not what you are asking for. Take a nap by yourself.

I knew that you were going to try to touch me. I heard the bell ringing in that empty head of yours.

You are really a helpful person, you did not get my bowling ball, but when it comes to tit feeling you are always there.

You should have that thing cut off and maybe that small brain of yours would start working.

Then maybe you should not because that is where your brain is.

Forget it, I am just a maid around here and maids don't provide sexual favors, you don't get that from a maid or a servant.

What is wrong, what did I do, what is wrong, what did I do? What makes you think that you did something wrong?

You know what you did, It was something you have no business doing.

What is, "no, no". It is what ever is on your mind while you are creeping around me.

Don't expect me to do things with you and that means anything that your small mind is thinking about.

Do you ever leave anything alone?

I just said I don't want your money; I have nothing to sell, Jesus Christ!

Yes, I am a mean woman, irritable and nasty.

Yes, it is a nice air mattress but there is no need to try it out. Sample it; is that the word that you use?

Don't you have anything else in that small brain or yours?

I don't know what's in that small cone head of yours. I don't want anyone sleeping close to me. I don't care what husbands do, I don't want you poking me in the bed either.

You are sure not going to jump on my bones tonight, just because it is the first of the month.

I have a headache.

When will I feel better? I don't have a clue. I am going to feel bad all month and maybe until the next year.

I did not say once a month, I said once every five years.

You guys think of nothing but trying to make your disabled parts work, taking Viagra, you should just give it up.

No let's hug business; it is not tit touching time. You are the worst, they don't come any worse.

Don't put your hands on me, they are nasty and I know where they will go.

Marriage and sex don't go together. There are people who are married that don't have sex. They just have things in common, like talking and companionship.

Yes, I am talking about people who live on the planet earth.

You never heard of them, well, do you know everyone on the planet earth

No! You can't have any of that "thing." Anyway what is a "thing" I don't have a thing.

I am not going to be the source of your exercise.

Get sex off your mind, you were once a good looking man, now you are an old fart all bent over.

I am going to bed, if you want to go to sleep come on in, no fooling around.

You are a child, because all you look at is tits and they are for children and you are an old man.

Not only are you an old man, you are a dirty old man.

I really have a headache. Yes, I have had a headache for the past five years.

I think it is going away in the year 2025, my headache that is.

Why do you ask another question and when I answered no to the first question? You ask, "Why?" I answered your damn question and the answer is still no.

Why do you ask me to call you when I go to bed, what business is it of yours when I go to bed, anyway I go to bed to sleep and nothing else.

You are not unique you are weird.

Sleeping close to your husband is not a prerequisite to being married.

You equate closeness with love and it has nothing to do with love or sex, there is a difference you know.

No! I can't teach you what love is because everything that I try to teach you, you tend to over do it. So just forget it and continue the way you are.

It is all in your head, you were asleep last night before you hit the bed.

Just take a cold shower, or go find five fingers Mary. If she is not available, then try to do with out it.

You are the one that has no brains, or your brains are in your pants between your legs and all your thoughts come from there.

Don't you think that you might be slightly sick, anything to do with sex is constantly on you mind, you should get a life.

Why are you brushing you lap, not for me to sit on it, as if you have something to brush.

I am not wearing this sweater again, it gets too much attention from you, and it pops your eyes out.

Yes, I said something about your eyes, and stop calling me Jane, I am not Jane Mansfield.

That two letter word "No", really has you confounded.

You don't seem to grasp its meaning.

It has nothing to do with a headache or feeling sick. Here is what it means, "I don't want to, am not going to and nothing that you can give me or buy me will change my mind. So you can forget it, old man.

You were trying to touch my tits and almost fell because your brain started before your old body could react.

I might have what you want to take but it ain't for the taking.

Women are from Venus and men are from no where.

You are like an octopus, keep your hand to yourself.

I know what I want and I don't need you to give me any information as to what I want or don't want.

To you, marriage is just sex and a good screwing.

To you marriage is not meaningful conversation, friendship and closeness, just sex.

If they are on your body they are yours. If they are on my body they are mine. I don't claim anything on your body.

No! I don't want to sit in your lap… I would not want to sit in anyone's lap even J.C.

would you just quit; I am tired of you getting behind me.

How many times do I have to tell you that I don't have to announce when I am going to bed. I go to bed to get some rest and not to have someone jump all over my bones. Go back to your study and forget it.

People who give, always get, you don't have anything to give.

When you say, "I love you" touch you crotch.

No! I'm not wearing a bra because it hurts my back. I wish these were your tits then you would understand how women feel about them.

Touch my tits and I will kick you.

What's wrong! What's wrong! There must be something wrong and you know it because you have to ask a question like that after you pinch my butt.

There is a big bell that rings in your head before you reach out and touch me.

Your tape recorder brain says let me touch my wife and annoy her.

You don't have anything else to do, not with me anyway, so just forget it.

Find something else to do, do I ever look like I can't find something to do.

All you have to do is see a pretty girl and you go nuts, you live through you stupid eyes, you jerk.

It's insulting; you never comment on how good I look, it is always on my butt or by boobs. I don't need that type of compliment.

When was the last time that you complimented me on how smart I am?

What do you mean that smart doesn't count to a married man? So that is all that counts, sex and wine in any order.

I know that I am intelligent but with you it is always a compliment on my butt or my boobs.

A booty call! You want a booty call; you are too old and bent over for any type of booty call.

You are going to bed with me, that's a threat, that's a threat.

So you got my bowling ball for me what do you want a reward?

You could not do anything to make me feel good, give me a break.

Everything that you say to me has sexual overtones. Try to have a decent conversation for a change.

What you want or don't want makes no difference to me.

You are constantly talking about what you can do, who do you think you are and some kind of super guy?

I think that the only reason that you get me to fix your collar is so that you can feel my tits.

Next time fix your own damn collar.

So you went out and bought me candy, well that just takes care of the times that I have balled you.

Someone told you that you were affectionate, but you are not. You don't know how to be affectionate.

You might have paid for someone else's body, but not mine. When we got married you did not have a damn cent.

You are obsessed with sex and that is sick and boring.

When you hug me it is just to feel my big tits, otherwise you would not move from side to side.

You are not God's gift to women and you never were, have you got that?

Do you know what a bed is for, a bed is for sleeping and that is what I intend to do, go to sleep

Help me! Help me! Help me! That is all that I get from you. You should learn to do things for yourself. If you want other help ask five fingered Mary.

It is impossible to live with most men; they are self centered, dirty and think they should be screwed and waited upon.

Most of you guys love yourselves.

When you make your so called "love", I am just trying to get over the moment.

don't allow you to make love with me. I just allow you to have sex. I don't need it or want it.

Don't tell me what I am thinking; you don't know what I am thinking. I know what you are thinking and it is not worth mentioning.

Get a divorce, I would like to see what fool would live with you.

Why do you reach over and grab my hand, you know I don't like it and you do it just to annoy me.

I am going to bed to get a good nights' sleep, and not anything else, I have a headache. Get Mary to do it,

Make love! You don't have a clue as to what making love is all about.

Making love is caring and not just sex.

You are in love all right, in love with yourself.

You don't need to love me if that is the way you love, feeling my tits and pinching my butt, believe me. I can do without your type of love.

You pinch my butt one more time and get kicked in the teeth.

You hugged me and then asked how that was? Which means you did it for some type of evaluation.

I would not sit in your lap if you were dying, you can just forget it.

If you do something for me there has to be a reason. So I don't want you to do anything to me or for me.

My back does not need rubbing, you might like that but I consider it invasive, so lay off.

Whenever I am close to you, you pick on my body parts, my tits and my butt.

Get your mind out of the gutter, you sound like a broken record.

You don't want a hug, and you know that. You don't know what a hug is or how to hug. What you want is to cop a tit feel.

Your mother didn't have time too nurse you when you were a baby, she was to busy having babies, fifteen of them. Now you have a fixation on tits.

I am not you mother so get over it.

Put your hand on me and you are going to lose some fingers.

One day you will find yourself lying on the floor saying, "I can't believe she did this to me." Just keep on feeling my tits.

I am not interested in what you want; I really am not interested at all.

If you really want to insure my death just do what you're always trying to do, use your joystick.

That is why so many men are accused of rape. No! Does not mean maybe.

I don't know where you got that from. When a woman says no, that is just what she means.

Get that between your ears.

Oh! Stop brushing your lap, I am not going to sit on your lap, that is stupid.

You are not only old but your mind is in left field or someone's lap.

You would have noticed it if it had been a woman, that is the way you men are.

Where did I get those roses?

Some guy gave them to me; he had to rush out because he forgot it was Valentines Day.

Levitra might give you four hours but I don't want four minutes.

You know what women want; you are such an expert about women.

You don't know shit about what a woman wants. You just keep talking about it.

So if you don't think she was walking funny, why you are telling a lie with that stupid smile on your face.

I agree, you are a sorry number.

Just because I am your wife that doesn't mean that I have to give you a piece of pussy.

You really are romantic you call a woman a piece of pussy.

You can sleep on the sofa tonight.

You are something else.

A woman is the same as a man, the only difference is that a man has a thing that he wants to stick in any hole that he can find, and with anyone that he can find that will let him.

Women don't let men! It is the man's fault; they are the ones who always want to touch something, feel something or screw something.

Just don't touch me at the dinner table and I mean that.

No I am not going to give you a time to touch me.

I get tired of your conversation. Can't you ever think of anything but body parts?

You don't have a clue as to what love is, Love is comfort, conversation and caring. Love is not sex and sex is not love. That is to everyone but you.

You are a letch; a letch is someone who always ogles women, talking about what big tits they have.

Why do you ask questions like that, you are waiting for me to say, no? It is almost like a challenge.

Don't give me that, "I'm just."

I'm not talking about you making a choice; everyone knows what your choice would be, with your simple mind.

You can stay on your diet and do the exercises yourself.

There is no place in the Atkins Diet book that says you should get your exercise by jumping on someone's body.

You may as well take a walk; you are not going to get any exercise with me, go ride your bike.

Don't be silly, you always act so silly, you act like a teenager, and I really think that you are regressing. You don't need it. It's all in your mind.

Read my mind. No. You seem to be able to read everyone else's.

No not tonight, have you asked me how my back feels, you just think of yourself and what you want.

I don't want my back rubbed, get out of here, and leave me alone.

Think of how I feel sometimes and stop always thinking about sex.

I said "Don't touch my ears", I don't like it and that is just why you keep on doing it.

You don't know anything, all that is in your head is sex.

I am going to bed to sleep, that is what the bed is for.

You can come in there if you want to just don't disturb me.

It is always, "Let me feel your tits" in the guise of let me hug you.

You can thank me without touching me, you see with your eyes and not your hands.

I had to tell the kindergarten children that, and now I have to tell you.

Why do you keep asking me that, you know what the answer is going to be, no.

Yes, I am going to bed and I am going to sleep and nothing else.

You can come in there if you want to, just don't wake me up.

Why are you touching me, you have to touch me, why?

Don't touch me; it is all play with you.

You have no feelings; you look in my face to see how it annoys me. That is just what you are doing.

You can't focus on anything but my arms and my chest at dinner time, it is always at the dinner table.

When I told you that you never ask me how I feel, I didn't mean for you to ask me every five minutes.

You are doing that just to get on my nerves.

Do you know what day this is, or what year this is, it is not time, and anyway I said in five years. My back is hurting so you can forget it.

I don't want you touching my feet; you do it just because you know that I don't like it.

You are just being annoying. Go find something to do to keep you out of my hair.

I am just not interested in that, you and sex, that is all you have on your mind. There is more to life than sex.

What else is there? You go figure it out and leave me alone.

I told you once before, Damn the national average, I still say no.

You over did it with that national average shit when you were young, it's time to let it rest.

That is probably what is wrong with my back, you jerk.

How many times do I have to tell you that I don't want you to kiss my hand? Anyway you would not stop at kissing my hand, you would be feeling every part of my body and I mean my body.

I can't have a decent conversation with you because it is

always about sex. So old men need sex, well go some place and get it or use your hand.

You come in here and sit right on top of me, you are a nuisance. I don't think it is funny, move over. You think that is funny.

You really believe in that saying, "Reach out and touch someone" don't you.

You don't understand that it means touch someone's hand and not someone tits or butt.

A mistress tries to please because she gets money. I am a wife.

I get money no matter what, whether I please or not.

You aren't going to do anything; every time I ask you to do something you come up with, "I will do this if you do that" forget it.

No, I don't want a hug. Think about the last time you hugged me and make it the last time.

I said no, what does that mean to you.

I am not one of those women from your home town, when I say no, it means just that, hell no.

Sure the women in your home town made good wives.

Why didn't you marry one of then if they said no and meant maybe.

I am not one of them and you had better get use to it, dumb man.

I was young then; I am now old enough to know better.

Not tonight, it is not the night so you can turn over and just go to sleep and leave me alone.

No, thank you, I don't want a kiss.

You are nothing but a big phony with all that love shit.

You can forget your three minutes. It would take you three minutes to remove your pants.

I don't want your three minutes, so tonight you can just go to sleep and forget it.

Men are animals, animals, men are animals.

How many times do I have to tell you that I don't have to give notice as to when I'm going to bed?

I'm going to bed to rest and nothing else. You can forget your three minutes, two minutes or one minute.

You can not kiss me goodbye, you don't have a wife, and you just have someone that you can pick on.

No, I will not wait up for you, leave me alone. I will go to bed when I'm tired and not before.

Shut up, women don't just chuck it on men, and men should keep that thing in their pants.

All the trouble that you have had came because you can't keep that thing of yours in your pants where it belongs.

I have been in this house all day alone and in didn't miss you pawing me.

I didn't have to talk to someone without a vocabulary and it was truly wonderful.

Having a baby is nothing? You try having one.

You have four minutes for me, to do what; it would take you four minutes to get out of that chair.

I am thinking of you now and that is all you get, a nice thank you, so forget the rest.

No, thank you, I don't need any help with anything.

Why do you stay up so late? No, I don't want you to come to bed for me, I am going to sleep.

You can come in if you want to.

Stay up as long as you want to; just don't wake me up when you come to bed.

Get away and leave me alone, all this concern comes because I complained and not because you have any genuine feelings for me.

Pinching my butt is totally disrespectful, but that is the way you operate.

You don't think that your actions are abusive you, but they are.

How many times does someone have to say no to you, the word "No" does not register with you?

The word is "No".

There doesn't have to be a reason to do something nice for someone, that is the way you think. You want a reward for being nice.

You said to me, "Today is the fifteenth and I said the tenth, it isn't my fault that you can't keep up with the day of the month.

So you are out of luck, No you can't have a mulligan. You can go to sleep and forget it.

Is that your business, do you have a bra?

They should castrate old me like they do dogs.

They would live longer and their mind would be on other important things.

I have to protect my body and do this at the same time; there is someone who always wants to touch it.

Don't start, don't start, four days of peace and now I have to go through the touching of the arm and what is on your chest shit.

Why do you touch my tits if you know I don't want you too, you sicko.

You always come up with, "Let me kiss you", you are so full of yourself.

Are your kisses going to wake me from slumber, or make me rich?

I can't relax in this house because you always want something from me. I have a toe ache that is a cousin to a headache.

Anyone who puts up with someone like you should receive an award.

Find some one else to pick on if you are bored. I don't care what the women in Winton liked, they were stupid anyway.

With all the thought that you have given me today, I am supposed to conjure up feelings for you.

All you have to be is nice some of the time and you don't know how to be nice.

I don't want anything that you think you have, wish you had and know you have.

I'm going to bed to sleep and nothing else. It is not the fifteenth or the first of the month so leave me alone.

It has not been five years, you just can't count but it is going to be another five years, so just leave me alone.

Every time at the dinner table you have to comment on my blouse.

Go find some else to love, you simpleton. I don't want you to love me, not that you know what love is.

Some of you guys think you are superior to females but you can't do anything for yourself.

Go out of here and find a wife that you can sit close too, you piece of shit.

So you stopped making pots and ate dinner with me, put your hand on your shoulder, now pat.

Penis envy! I would never want that piece of meat hanging off me, it is just something that gets in the way and that you play with.

I would not want that thing hanging off me. I have enough hanging with my tits.

These tits are mine and are not for you to be looking at, playing with, touching or picking at. You do not have the back pains from them and I do.

Try to find something to do except pick on me. Try to find something constructive to do with your time and your hands.

Go find a wife to hold hands with, I don't want you holding my hands, you don't even know how to hold hands properly.

If you know so much about what the women in Winton, where you grew up, did or didn't do, why don't you go there and marry one and leave me in peace.

How do you know what husbands do, have you been around a husband, I think not, you would not know a husband if you saw one.

You have two brains and one is more powerful than the other, the most powerful brain is in your pants. It does most of your thinking.

I don't know what the other brain is used for; I guess it is just to make my life miserable.

The only help you can give me is to stop sitting in this room with me and asking me to come to bed with you.

I should not have gotten a large king size bed, I should have gotten twin beds and then you would not be able to poke me.

You sleep too close to me and I am tired of you poking me.

So it is Christmas Eve, what does that mean? I am going to bed to sleep and that is the end of that.

I don't give a damn if it is Christmas, you get nothing here. I am going to bed and I am going to sleep.

I don't care what husbands do.

You get what you pay for and you did not pay for anything. When I met you did not have a pot or a window. So you did not buy anything.

You would think that part of your body would be tired by now.

No! I will not call you when I go to bed, I go to bed to sleep and not to be bothered and poked by you.

I am going to bed you can come in there if you want to sleep but that is all, get it.

I have said to you a hundred times that I will not tell you when I am going to bed. What difference would it make if you knew when I am going to bed? I am going to bed to sleep and not to be poked or put upon.

Go away, I am not feeling well.

I am going to feel better in 1902, so time has to go around and come back.

This is my body and I don't have to give it away to anyone.

All you know how to do is look at my chest, just keep your hand off me.

What wife school did you attend that told you that wives are only to be picked on and put upon, rubbed on and nailed?

The only school that you attended was in that stupid town of Winton, North Carolina where you grew up with your no good father.

We were not put on this earth for the pleasures of men. Who do you think you are anyway?

That is passive aggressive, because you sit here in front of me and drink wine, and then have the nerve to ask me for sex, you are a sick man.

Stop it, you keep your hands off me. I get sick and tired of you always picking at me.

I don't care to, if you don't mind and I don't care to even if you do mind!

Go away, go away! I don't think you are funny.

If that is all you have to talk about, then leave the room and leave me alone. I am too old to think about it, leave me alone.

Do it, that is all that is on that small mind of yours, shit head.

I am the kind of wife a man like you deserves.

I think that I am better than you deserve.

Put that in your pipe and smoke it.

Waking me up at three in the morning with your cold feet that is down right evil.

I don't have time to want anything, you are always there to shove it on me, give me a break.

Go play with five fingered Mary and leave me alone.

A dirty old man would pick up on that.

Did you hear the silence. I can't have a conversation with you, it always ends up the same way, sex.

You had better live with what you had in the past because you aren't going to get any in the future.

I don't think your mother nursed you when you were a baby because you are obsessed with tits.

Let me love you, I know what that means and so do you.

Don't put your hands one me, they are dirty, everything that you like to touch is up in my chest.

Try to remember that I am married to you. I know all the tricks to your trade. Smoke that in that pipe of yours.

You are constantly asking me to exercise. I do not need the type of exercise that you have in mind. I do not need you bouncing all over me.

I just wanted to tell you that I'm going to bed; there is no need for you to come in there. I am going to go to sleep and nothing else.

If you want to go to sleep, you are welcome to come in there.

I swear you are the incarnation of dirty Dick your father, with that nasty smile on your face.

Your brain doesn't work properly. We are watching television and you reach out and try to feel my tits. You are really something special. You did not buy and pay for anything. When I met you did not have two pennies to rub together.

You are sick, sick, sick. You are the coldest man in the entire world barring none.

Don't be a nuisance, why do you do things like that. I don't want a kiss or a hug, both of those have strings attached to them.

Did you lose something over here, you are always reaching and grabbing.

Maybe next year, at your age you only need it about once every other year if you need it then.

Its all in your head, go take a cold shower.

The reason that you can't think, remember anything or find anything is because your brains are in your pants.

As usual, the nature of your conversation is either sex or pottery and I am not interested in either.

No! I am not going to ever play wife again.

You can't hold a conversation, you always have to bring it around to something stupid.

There is nothing gentle about you, for you that gentle stuff is just not done.

Look with your eyes and not your hand, keep your hands off me please.

With you it is always, "I just, I just... I just what?

No, I don't want a kiss, all you want to do is feel me, go do what you were doing.

Get away from me cat, you're like the damn man in this house, you are always rubbing something.

Yes, I read Ann Landers, that man is a pig, like you, he thinks sex is his God given right. Men just don't understand.

Why do you do the things that you do, you have to be touching and feeling all the time. No one should have to put up with the likes of you.

I don't want your hands on me and I don't want to kiss you, that mustache and beard looks like a vagina, and you come up with, are you going to bed? I'm coming in there with you. You come in there all you like

but you are not going to flop all over me, get that through your head.

Do you want to be a pain in the neck this evening,

go mind your own business and leave me alone.

Your conversation is so boring, its either pottery or sex

and I have lived with pottery for forty years and sex longer than that and I am sick of both.

Stop calling me Jane, I am not Jane Mansfield. Jane Mansfield was a blond with big tits. I am just a black woman with big tits.

I am going to bed by myself, so don't come in and start poking me.

Who do you think you are, you have snow on your roof.

You have had your monthly share of love so leave me alone.

It would take you more than ten minutes to remove your pants, so forget it. It would be more like two hours or two days.

Every once and a while but this is not once and a while.

Stop lying, why do you lie like that? It has not been ten years and if has what difference does it make?

I took my bra off because my shoulders hurt and all you can think about is what the view does for you. You really are a piece of work.

What are you trying to say, "You brought me candy as a incentive?"

Well you wasted your money, I have a headache. It is a headache that will last a long time, maybe for the next two months or more.

You probably didn't buy it, put that on your list. Where you write all that crap.

Me, let you fool with my sore arm, I am not crazy!

You just want to help me with my arm so that you can feel my tits, no thank you.

Pull my arm straight and don't touch here.

The therapist stands when she does my arm and yet you sit.

Are you trying to show concern, forget it, it is not in your nature.

I am always going to say, No! No! No!

If it is not something you can do by yourself, it doesn't look like you are going to get it any help.

If I died today you would have someone else in this house within an hour.

I don't give a damn how young she would be, help your self and die with a smile. I'll bet they would not be able to close the coffin.

I am not an exercise machine, you do it for yourself, to yourself, bouncing all over me.

You want to make love with me or do you just want to have sex.

Yes, there is a difference, not that it matters to you.

I know I have a headache and I will have a headache for the next thirty years.

You ask me why women always show cleavage, it is the same with you men, always showing your biceps and your washboards.

No, I don't want to see your washboards because all I would see is a big stomach and two tits.

There is no need to come in here. I am getting ready to turn off the lights, the television, and everything else. You are right, I turned everything off two years ago.

Why don't you sleep on your side of the bed? You move over on my side because it is warm and you can poke me. Your side will warm up in a few minutes.

I don't care if husbands sleep close to their wives.

How do you know what husbands do? You are not one and that father of yours was not one either.

The only thing that your father taught you was how to fish. He could not teach you to be a husband because he was not one himself.

Yes, the movie is called, "Consenting Adults" and no, I am not a consenting adult.

You had better get out of here before you lose your pecker or should I say poker.

When are you going to act your age old man? Turn over and go to sleep.

Last night you slept all over me and I did not get any rest. I wish you would stay on your side of the bed. I don't have space to even turn over.

Why do you keep asking me the same question over and over? You are always going to get the same answer. I really don't think that brain of yours is working. When I say no, it means no and not maybe.

On Writing

> The moving finger writes; and, having writ,
> Moves on; not all thy piety nor Wit
> Shall lure it back to cancel half a Line,
> Nor all thy Tears wash out a Word of it.
>
> *Rubaiyat of Omar Khayyam*

You can write anything you want to in that silly book. No one in the world would write a book on fussing and nagging but you.

Whenever I make a remark, you start writing.

They can't say that you plagiarized your dumb book, no one would write that crap

You want to write about me and want me to get you a pen and paper, fat chance.

You don't have to keep writing that damn book, it is finished, you have written enough shit as it is.

Every time I open my mouth and say anything you have to write it down, I am going to stop talking.

Send it to Dr. Phil, he will just think that you are crazy to write that kind of shit and he will see what I have to put up with and that you are a blooming idiot.

My husband the grump, here you go again with that damn journal of yours. You write down my words but I am not supposed to see them. The whole thing is one dumb adventure.

Yes, you are a grumpy person; sometimes you are grumpy with me and all you know how to do is write your stupid notes.

You are insane; you come in here with that dumb poem to justify how you feel about publishing that stupid book.

I don't say anything about you for your stupid book; anyway there are no words to describe you and what you are.

No! I didn't throw out what you wrote. I would not want the garbage man to see that junk.

Don't write that while we are eating. If you can't remember what I said it must not be important enough to write down.

I am going to do this. I am going to do that. You are not going to do anything except write those damn notes all over the place.

You are going to write that shit then spell it yourself or get a dictionary.

You write down ever word that comes out of my mouth, don't you have anything else to do? Go make some pots in that dirty shop of yours.

Sure, I am scared to say that and I am tired of you writing down my every word.

The stupid book is going to be really redundant and the reason is that you still have all of your bad habits and they have not changed.

You don't need another sheet of paper, use the back of that one.

Would you like for me to close this cabinet door. Write that down, write down that every morning I find the cabinet door sitting wide open.

I don't care for your book writing. I will not write a preview for

it. I think it is down right insulting, writing down what people say without their consent. It is down right stupid.

I don't want to see what you wrote, it is shitty anyway.

I can be kind to you, but it is hard, every time I open my mouth you write something down.

No! I didn't put those pads by the telephone for you to write your shit on.

That is all that you do. Write that shit down, you can't keep up with what day it is. I told you that it was Labor Day and there would be no mail and you went out to get the mail anyway, open your ears.

Use the back of the pad for your stupid notes; you waste lots of pads doing that nonsense.

Everyone will know that you have your shoes on the wrong foot and that your elevator doesn't go pass the first floor.

I am sitting in the study and watching television. No! Please, I don't need any help, just stay out of my way and write your stupid crap.

Who do you think is going to buy a book of insulting remarks written by a man who deserves them?

Except someone who is down right nasty and mean.

Notice how everything reverts back to you. No matter what I say you make it a part of you and your conversation, and your notes, I guess you can't help it.

You and your notes, you write notes on anything, do you realize that you are a pain in the ass.

You should bring a pad to write your silly notes on.

I am dealing with a ding bat, a real ding bat.

I will not sit in here with you; all you want to do is write something stupid on that pad.

I put those pads there by the phone, go to the garbage can and get something to write on. That is what you are writing, garbage.

We can't have a meaningful conversation. You have to write everything in that damn book, forget it.

I hate to put these pads here because they end up for you to write your crazy notes on.

I have a book for you to read, it is called "An Unquiet Mind." It is for those people who talk to themselves all the time.

You can write anything that you want as long as I don't have to sign it.

However, I think you are rude and evil.

How many times do I have to tell you that I write and read, only things that interest me?

Why do you have to write something down as soon as I say it? Can't you remember?

No! You can't remember, you have CRS {Can't remember shit}, and you are a ding bat.

There you go writing shit again.

You are constantly writing down everything that I say, is what I say that interesting?

You don't deserve a reward every time you do something for me, write that down.

Every time I open my mouth you get a pen and paper and start writing.

You are going to make yourself late, writing all those crazy notes about what I am saying.

I will not repeat what I said because I don't want it written down by you for that stupid damn book.

Every time I open my mouth you start writing, I am beginning to resent it.

I have no intentions of correcting your stupid book, get someone else to proof read it.

It really takes nerve to write that crap in my face. You are writing your dumb notes with me sitting here.

Keep writing your junk down, that is retarded.

Write that shit down, I don't care.

You used my paper for your dumb notes, for God's sake, I married a child.

OK, send that crap to anyone that you want to and they will think that you have lost your mind and know that you stopped at first base.

Anyone will think that you are crazy to write that kind of crap. They will sympathize with the poor lady that has to live with a loony.

Never mind, forget it and just write your shit for your book.

I don't care what you put on that paper; everyone will see what a blooming idiot you are.

Go write on your paper, "deputy dog."

Go write that in your silly book.

Just sit there and write all that shit on the paper. I am going to take you to the first insane asylum that I see and have you committed.

You want me to answer so that you can write it down, well, write that you are totally self serving.

I am going to write a book about you and you know what my book is going to have in it, sex, food and wine.

No, you live here so I don't live alone. I have a thorn in my bed of roses, You are that thorn.

What would you do without me? You would have nothing to write down or write about.

Get your own damn pen and paper.

These pads are for messages and not for you to write your shit on.

Every time I look for writing pads, you have put them someplace with your notes all over them.

I would not have enough paper to write all the stupid things that you do and say.

Please don't write on those things, I am tired of putting note pads out here.

I really don't understand it. Write down all the notes you want to, I really don't care.

Dr. Phil would come in here and see all that shit that you write down and ask why do you put up with that.

Nothing!! Write that in your book and everyone will know that you purchased the farm and tripped over your shoe laces.

No! I will not read it over carefully, write that down.

I put the pads our here for notices, not for you to write your stupid notes on.

I make a remark and you start writing. Who do you think wants to read that shit that you are putting on paper? I surely don't want to read it.

No! I will not read it over carefully. Put that on your list.

Every time I open my mouth you write something stupid down, I would rather say nothing at all. When are you going to quit writing those dumb notes?

Leave me alone about things like pads and pencils, go out and buy your own for your dumb note pads and stay out of my office.

Every time I open my mouth you grab a pen and start writing crap that no one wants to read.

I'm beginning to get annoyed with the whole thing.

I'm ignoring you.

The notes that you write down are really insane, do you know that?

Anyone who writes down these silly notes is insane.

There is nothing to write on, try keeping it in that small brain of yours so it will get wet with pee. You know where your brains are.

When I go out, I leave you a note. Does it ever occur to you to do the same thing?

Don't write that down, all right, all right, forget it.

Why can't you get your own pads?

The stuff that I say is for you and not some stranger.

Get your own pad, you are so full of yourself, I swear you are full of it.

Are you going to take the entire pad, and then we will have nothing to write on.

Write whatever you want to, I still say it is stupid.

Spend more time trying to keep up with your stuff rather than writing a lot of shit down.

I will give you more of something to write later today, you pitiful man.

Why don't you get a note book and stop using up all of our pads.

Get your own poison pen.

Were you thinking of me or just bored? Put that in your book, everything else crazy goes in it.

Why do you bring this letter to me this late in the evening to read over?

I don't see that well this late in the evening and I make mistakes. Read it your damn self.

Yes, I am allowed to make mistakes. Lord knows you make your share of them.

Put this in your book, "You are the grinch who stole Christmas.

One would think that you were writing the great American novel, considering the zeal and zest that you put into it.

You come in here and start writing on things.

You write on anything that has a flat surface on it.

You don't need to write anymore of that shit, the damn book is finished.

You can publish the damn book, I don't care. You will not embarrass me; you will embarrass your self. It is living proof that you are a blooming idiot.

I have no idea where your writing pad is. I try to keep things off the table where I am trying to eat.

Do you have to write that large. You could put more shit on that paper if you wrote smaller. I forget, you can't see or hear, you old man.

Why can't you take one sheet at a time from the telephone pads? Those pads are placed there for others to use and not just for you. I am others, Mr. Looney.

The Office and supplies

Indeed, indeed, Repentance oft before I swore,
But was I sober when I swore?
And then came Spring, and Rose - in - hand
My thread - bare Penitence apieces tore.

Rubaiyat of Omar Khayyam

The cleaning lady is coming in the morning would you please clean up your office.

I don't give a damn what you hired the cleaning lady to do. No one is going to come in my house and find it a mess. I told you that before, remember {CRS}.

All the equipment that you have in this office and only half of it works. The rest of the equipment just sits there doing nothing.

What did you get from the common store {my office}? So you are using nothing! When will it dawn upon you to buy your own supplies?

You still claim that you are in tune with the universe because you are disorganized. There is something wrong up there, your clock stopped before the hour.

You are totally disorganized and can't remember anything or do anything right.

I could not live like you. I could not go through life being so disorganized, never knowing which end is up or where anything is located. You spend too much of your life looking for things, it would drive me crazy.

Don't use pads on my desk to write your stupid notes on, get pads from your office if you can find them in that mess that you have on your desk.

If you kept your office in order you would be able to find things and not always be looking in my office.

In my office I am surrounded by things that are important to me. In your office you are surrounded by junk, you have nothing that is important to you.

It is called taking care of things and putting thing where they belong so that one can find them when they need them.

If you going to put that wet glass on my desk, put something under it.

You are really sloppy; you come in here and make a mess of my desk.

My office is not a pigsty like yours and I want to keep it neat and in order.

I am really happy that you found out what was wrong with your computer, now you can get Pogo on it. There is no reason for you to go in my office and use my computer so stay out of it.

There is some scientist going around looking for germs in offices and found lots of them. He has not been in your office. He would find that his instruments would go off the scales if he did.

You just don't understand how to use gadgets. All phones come that way, you will have to get use to it.

You went in my office, what did you take out of it? Whatever it was, please put it back and buy your own supplies.

Even if you buy them you will not be able to find them in your office, Mr. Entropy.

How did you know that was in my office?

That man goes through my stuff all the time and then says, "I know where to find the things that I need."

Stay out of my office looking for things, there is nothing in there that belongs to you.

What you need you will find at Staples or Wal-mart, not in my office.

So you are in tune with the universe, big deal, if the universe wants disorder you are the prime candidate.

There is a burn mark on the carpet in my office did you put it there.

Forget it; there are no gremlins, fairies or people from outer space living in this house.

There are only two people living here and I don't smoke. One of these days you are going to burn the damn house down with that stupid pipe.

I don't smoke a pipe or anything else so I did not put the burn mark in the carpet in my office.

Do you wonder why I don't want you in my office?

You volunteer the use your copier for everyone and everyone's mother, that is why your expensive copier cartridge doesn't last.

As soon are your copier runs out, into my office you come to use my copier.

One copier cartridge would last me for five years and you go through one in a month doing work for everyone but yourself.

Don't come in my office and use my copier, just keep on buying those expensive copier cartridges and using them for everyone and everyone's brother.

You come in my office because you can never find anything in that pigsty that you call an office.

Try buying your own supplies and you would not need to come in my office and steal them.

If you purchase them you would not keep up with them anyway.

I want you to stay out of my office. When I got up this morning my papers and other things were all over the floor.

The rocks from my little water fall were all over the floor. What did you do to my office? You never clean up the mess that you make.

Do you ever consult your calendar? I just wonder if it was worth putting on your desk, it has crap all over it.

You should see your desk calendar that I purchased for you, it's appalling; there is shit all over it.

Why do you come in my office and move my pocketbook and then sit down. There is nothing in here that belongs to you.

Your office is a mess as usual.

There is no point in thinking that you are going to be organized.

You stay in bed until eleven and most of your day is gone. You get up and come in my office and ask what I am doing. I am minding my business.

No, I don't stay in bed late, that has never been my thing. I don't know why you expect me to do it now. Is there a reason for you wanting me to stay in bed all day? I get up and work in my office; it is peaceful and serene until you come in.

Why do you pick at my things, there is nothing in this office that belongs to you.

I don't borrow things, I use my own things and I always put them back in their place where I can find them when I want them.

I purchased my computer because your desk is always cluttered and covered with who knows what.

Whenever I sit at your desk I start cleaning it.

Everything around you is junkie and cluttered, you make a mess wherever you are.

I don't understand how one person can be so disorganized. How do you live with yourself, you never know where you put anything.

This is awful, look at the mess that you spilled on your desk. No! I don't want you to clean it up, you would use one of my dishcloths and that is not what dishcloths are used for.

Dishcloths are use for dishes, not for a mess like this, get out of my way.

Why don't have a special place to put the things you need, Lord only knows. That is something that you should learn to do. Then you would not always be asking, "Where is my, Where is my?"

Stay out of my office, "Need some tape", like you purchased tape.

Get out of my office and don't take my paper, get your own writing paper. That kiss will not change anything. It is still my office and my paper.

My desk is never a mess like this, why can't you keep your desk clean? I asked a question, do you have an answer?

You will never go into anyone's office and find it the way yours is.

Yes! I use the hunt and peck system when I type or the Columbus system, as you call it. {Find a key and land on it} but it gets the job done.

I don't talk about the errors that you make when you type, like leaving the "s" of words and other errors.

Go back in your office and stop watching me play computer games. I don't pester you or watch you when you are playing that dumb spades game.

You are no good at playing games anyway that is why you want to watch and criticize me and call the games stupid.

You make excuses with that crap about you being in tune with nature and it is just an excuse to keep your place like a pigsty.

I am going to purchase something for your damn desk. I will get it organized if it is the last thing that I do… I am going to fix that stupid mess, there are papers all over the place.

I am determined to get you organized. If I succeed then maybe you will stay out of my office.

There are papers all over your desk and the floor how do you ever find anything. That I will never understand. It is definitely not normal behavior.

I purchased a calendar pad for your desk and tried to put it in some order. See if you can keep it that way for an hour or so.

I put that calendar on your desk and got up this morning and found it covered with crap. You just can't teach old dogs new tricks.

I don't want to hear about that entropy shit, it is just your way of justifying your behavior.

You are in tune with the universe; well the universe is one disorganized, dysfunctional place.

So you know what nature wants, think of all the people in the world and then decide if you are unique. I don't think so and neither does Mother Nature.

I don't see how anyone can work around a mess like this.

It is no wonder that you can't find anything in your office. Just stay out of my office, there is nothing in there that belongs to you.

Does my office tell you something, that women are neater than men?

You are not a neat person, why would you even think about neatness or make a statement about neatness, you are not neat.

You went in my office because I could not find my computer mouse. I found it in your office. My mouse does no work on your system.

Why don't you try new batteries in that cordless mouse? It might just work on your computer.

If your mouse was not working the correct thing to do would be to put in new batteries not destroy the place.

The next time you take a book out of my bookcase please leave the case like you found it, is that so very difficult for you to do?

You don't feel comfortable when things are neat and tidy do you?

You have finished with my pen, please put it back where you found it. Then I will not have to look for it.

You never directly answer a question; you always have some dumb remark just to change the subject. Get a grip on life.

Noisy computer! Welcome! You have mail! Huh? Get a damn hearing aid. I can hear your computer four rooms away.

Why do you have to have the sound so high on your computer? I can hear it in the other room. What you need is a hearing aid, old man. Many old people, like you, use hearing aids and there is nothing wrong with wearing one.

You are so disorganized; I don't know how you live with your self.

Who do you think cleans up your mess, the good fairy?

You are totally discombobulated.

Do you have an aversion to being organized?

Papers are everywhere on your desk. I don't understand how anyone can live that way. It is not normal for anyone to live like that.

I swear I can have no privacy, you just go through my stuff.

People call you to fix their computer not because you know so much about computers, I have watched you and all you do is fiddle around until you find what is wrong.

I can't believe the people who ask you to work on their computers.

I don't believe that you know a damn thing about computers and how they function.

I don't want you to teach me how to use the computer. I will learn all I need to know by myself.

Go in and clean your office I don't care if you are paying the cleaning lady to do it. No one is going to come in and find my house a dirty mess and that means your office too.

I don't care what you paid for, just go in and clean your office and be quiet. This is my house and I am not going to have people talking about how dirty it is.

Every morning when I get up I find your desk a mess. Do you make any effort to clean your mess?

Why can't you be neat and tidy like your friend Charlie? Yes, I would like to live with him. At any rate his place would not be a pigsty.

I don't understand why you are over here in my office opening my things. There is nothing in my office that belongs to you, so just get out of here.

What happened to the scissors that I had in the desk drawer in my office.

There is a place called "Staples" and they have office supplies to sell.

If you want supplies you should go to the store and buy them. Where do you get off thinking that my office is some damn supply store?

My office is not a supply store; try Staples or your favorite store Wal-mart and buy your own supplies.

You used my fingernail clippers and they are not where they belong, did you put them back where you found them?

I purchased thirty nine dollars worth of stamps for my office and you used most of them.

Why don't you purchase your own stamps, you are too cheap.

I was going into your office and putting your desk in order each morning, but what's the use of doing it. You just make a mess of it again. There are papers all over the place.

When you finish working, is it too much trouble to put your papers in one pile?

That is why you can never find anything in your office, it is a mess. The first thing out of your mouth is, "where is my".

Back in my office again, when are you going to realize that my office is not a supply house?

Have you ever bought any supplies for yourself or are you just waiting for me to buy them.

Sometimes I think that you hit a home run but never reached first base or the ball hit you in the head and addled your brain.

Purchase your own supplies, stamps and other items needed in your office, I don't run an Office Depot, Staples or Wal-mart in my office

Even if you had supplies in your office you would not be able to find them in all that mess.

Do you want "THE" Christmas wrapping paper that you purchased or do you want "MY" Christmas wrapping paper that I purchased. That is the paper that I purchased to wrap my gifts. That is the Christmas wrapping paper that I purchased with my money.

Where did you learn to wrap Christmas gifts? It is very painful watching you wrap paper around those gifts.

Even if someone is just going to take the paper off it should still be neatly done or not done at all.

You are not wrapping gifts you are just rolling the paper around them.

Why don't you just put your gifts in a brown paper bag, I think they would look nicer.

Have you been in the my office where you keep "your" supplies?

You are in my office with your mess and your dirty pipe.

I like the way you work on the computer, instead of reading the directions, you just fiddle with it until it works.

Why do you work in such disorder and don't give me that entropy shit, I don't want to hear it? It really means nothing anyway.

So the universe strives for disorder, well who ever created it should be really proud of you.

I put the flashlights back in my office, where you found them, stay out of my office. Buy your own supplies and then lose them.

You look at what I have and wonder how I can keep it so nice and neat. You don't have anything and what you do have, you make a complete mess of it. I like my things nice and neat.

I see someone has been searching in my office for scissors again. I know because they are not in the special place where I keep them.

I see my bags are already being used and I just got them from the store.

So you see how neat and clean your desk is. I cleaned it while you were gone; try to keep it that way. Oh! Just forget I said that.

There is some motive behind everything that you do; you do things just to irritate me. I think you are disorganized just so you can get on my nerves.

Are you going to put that glue back when you finish with it?

You go in my office because it is organized and things can be found. Why don't you buy the things that you need.

My office is not your supply house. It is not a place for you to go for your office needs; there are stores for that purpose.

You might be more in tune with the universe but you are still disorganized.

What a nasty house, you sit at the kitchen table and do everything from glazing your pots to writing a letter.

Why don't you have a place to do those things? It is because there is no space on your desk to do anything.

Go into your pottery shop if you want to work on your pots, the kitchen is my space.

You sit in front of that computer for an hour, do I complain? I don't understand how you can complain about anything that I do.

What is my tape doing on the floor of your office? You were going to put it back. I bet you were going to put it back.

That tape would be on the floor of your office forever.

You go in my office and remove my things and never put anything back where they belong. You could find your own tape if you had a special place for your supplies.

It is none of your business whether I read those books or what books I read, they are in my office, not yours.

Don't be sorry just clean up your mess. I had to do it for the children and I am not going to do it for you.

I can't be raising another house full of children.

You don't feel comfortable when things are neat, tidy and organized in your office do you?

You stated that you were going to keep your office clean, look at that mess.

You are so damn disorganized, if you purchased supplies and put them in your office would not be able to find them in that mess.

You cleaned your office. I'm thrilled to death, that you cleaned your damn room for yourself, thanks a lot.

Unbelievable, one day later and your study is a damn pig's pen.

I notice how you sneak in my office when I am not around to steal my supplies.

Your office is the nastiest room in the world; you have your shit everywhere.

I don't need your help with my computer so just leave.

If I do it wrong it is my computer so don't worry about it. I will teach myself how to use it.

You are a poor computer teacher and you wonder why I don't ask you any questions about the computer.

I don't ask you questions about my computer because you don't know how to answer or fix it.

You always try to make me look as if I don't know what I am doing, that is why I don't ask you any questions about the computer.

There are many spots on the rug in your office if you cleaned them up as soon as they occurred, the rug would be easier to keep clean.

Your magnifying glass! This magnifying glass has my name on it and it came out of my office.

When I was in Smithtown I was given a bowling pin, when we got to North Carolina, you claimed it and had your name engraved on it. That magnifying glass has my name on it and it was in my desk drawer.

What about the study did you straighten it up? Try to remember that the cleaning lady comes today.

You aren't tearing that up are you, you tore the other box up that the slides came in. Don't you know how to open boxes?

Where did you get that manila folder? It's mine; just put it back in my office where you found it.

Try to remember that my office is not a supply store for you.

What are you looking for in my office? How many times do I have to tell you that my office is not a store or an office supply warehouse?

When are you going to start buying the office supplies that you need and keep track of them?

Where did you get the stamps placed on the letters that you put in the mail box?

How can you come in my office and steal my stamps, and then removed the end so that I will not notice that they are gone.

Have you ever purchased stamps, the United States Postmaster does not live or sleep in my office and my office is not a Post Office or a place to purchase stamps.

If you want stamps buy them or at least ask for them or purchase them yourself. Try to remember if you can, that my office is not a United States Post Office.

I found my rolodex on you desk this morning. I was looking for it and it was not where I always keep it. I wonder how it got there since you always return things that you borrow from my office because you can never find anything in your office. My rolodex must have walked into your office and placed itself on your desk.

You keep your addresses on your computer so why would you need my rolodex. It is because you are too lazy to open your computer and find the addresses that you need.

The next time you take something from my office please have the courage or whatever it takes to replace it where you found it. Thank you.

Do you want me to make a rolodex for you and record all the addresses, forget it? It would do no good, in a day or so you would not be able to find it anyway.

Stay out of my office, if and when you need something in my office ask me for it. Better still go out and buy the things that you need in your office and spend the rest of your life looking for them.

I was looking for my scissors. My scissors were not where I keep them. I found them in your office where they do not belong. Why don't you use your own scissors or is it that you can't find them?

I think you are just too lazy to look for scissors or anything else in that mess in your office.

Fussing

> Fussing requires a sense of humor, something you do not possess. I have a quick wit, you do not, so you can forget about learning to fuss.

Oh thou who didst with pitfall and with Gin
Beset the Road I was to wander in,
Thou wilt not with predestination round
Enmesh me, and impute my fall to sin.

Rubaiyat of Omar Khayyam

You always leave your shit for me to clean up. When are you going to learn to clean up after yourself? Who is going to clean the ashes off you when you get to hell?

It is easy to make snide remarks to you because you open yourself up to them.

The normal workday starts at eight and ends at five but you do not get up until twelve, except to play golf.

Men do not care about their children, they are too wrapped up in themselves.

Fussing has a sense of humor, something that you do not possess.

I have a quick wit, you do not, so you can forget about learning to fuss.

I need to sneeze and make some noise so that someone will know that I do not feel well.

I think sometimes that I live with a pig.

Neither you nor your son knows how to close a door or turn off a light.

Your elevator has not left the basement in a long time, in other words, you are two cans short of a six pack.

How do you know how wives are supposed to behave, you have never been one or seen one. I'm not a wife I am a maid who gets nailed.

With you, it's always the same thing, we come to the dinner table and sit down and you reach out and touch my arm, then you ask for a hug. The same thing each day, it is enough to drive a sane person crazy.

I am going to buy you some silicon so that you can play with it and I am going to attach an arm so that you will have something to touch, then you will be able to leave me alone.

That is the way it always is, call this person, do that, do this, one would think that you have a servant or a secretary.

Why is your bowling ball still on the kitchen floor, sure you were going to move it? Sometime next year, just put it where it belongs.

Do not do things at the spur of the moment; take time to consider what you want to do.

When you have nothing to do you are a nuisance, it is then that you hang around and bother me.

You are just like a potato sitting there like a big lump and I have to go all the way around you.

Don't you think that you go over board with that, how some one looks?

I did not ask for any help, help yourself.

Thank you doesn't help, unless you say please first.

You don't know how to do anything but you know how to ask me to do something.

You are still opening that drawer looking for your socks and they haven't been in that drawer for years. In fact, I change them around ten years ago.

The furniture was moved six months ago and you are still bumping into it, get a grip on life.

Do you love this house? If you do, spend some time taking care of it. I don't mean hire another house cleaner.

I don't mean hiring someone to do the work that you are supposed to do.

You are so infantile. You are like a two year old, slurp, slurp, that is rude.

I missed you. Did I say that?

Oprah doesn't fuss with Stedman because she has money, plenty of it. She also has some one to clean up his bad habits.

I was going to clear up the mess you made. You were going to clean it up. I know, but it would be tomorrow, the next day, the next week, or the next year.

At least I write something down as to where I am going. That is not like someone that I know.

I wake up and have no idea where you are, not that it matters a damn.

You just don't want to see me rest do you? I sit here and close my eyes and you ask me some question. I allow you to sit and rest why can't you do the same for me?

Take it out, don't put it back, don't close drawers, that is the way things are around here.

You have been on my back all day, get out.

Do you want me to turn off the light in here since you are no longer in this room?

You don't put things back where they belong, "I was." That is your answer to everything. "I was."

I don't have to do things just to please other people. I just do things to please myself.

The dishwasher works OK; I come home and find dishes in the sink. You could have loaded the dishwasher since I was gone all day.

You will never learn to fuss properly. You have to move your hand and you talk too fast. That is not the way to fuss properly.

I don't babble when I fuss, I talk slowly and I don't move my hands and my body.

You don't see me moving my hands and talking so fast that I can't get the words out; I calmly say what I have to say. Maybe it requires something special like mother wit to fuss properly, something that you do not have. Just go in the other room and forget it, you are a lost cause.

Forget trying to learn to fuss properly, you will never learn, it takes to much brainpower.

No! you don't have the knack to fuss because it takes intelligence and wit of which you do not have.

It does not take an intelligent person to make intelligent quips, it takes a sharp person and you are not a sharp person.

You will never learn to fuss properly. Fussing must take some special talent, which you do not have; I think it is called mother wit. Just go to the other room and be quiet.

You are just jealous because you can't talk like that.

You get all tongue-tied and start shouting. You will never be able to fuss properly.

I can't teach you to fuss because you do not have the necessary mother wit and intelligence to do it properly and practice will not help you so forget it.

Shut up, learn to fuss and do it properly or just shut up.

Why do you get so excited when you talk, can't you control yourself, you had better learn to do it.

Some people have no wit, which is necessary to fuss properly, and I or no one else can teach you how to do it. You are a slow learner.

No one can teach you to fuss properly because you don't have any wit and you surely don't have a sense of humor.

When you try to fuss you sound like a blooming idiot. Forget it, you will never learn to fuss properly. It requires too much intelligence and wit.

Why do you have to shout when you try to fuss, I don't do stupid things like that? I just say what I have to say and that is the end of it.

I have tried my last time to teach you how to fuss. You don't have the wit or the brains to do it properly.

Why, because it is a smart thing to do and you can't think of anything smart to say?

If you have nothing to say that is meaningful, keep your trap shut.

You don't have the ability to make the necessary retort required for many situations.

I will never be able to teach you to fuss properly.

What else did you have to do that was so important you could not help me bring the packages in from the car?

Someone went into the refrigerator and left it open, there are just two of us in this house and I did not do it.

I don't know what in the hell is wrong with you, you are a sick man. Why turn the ice tray upside down to get to the ice. Now the ice is all over the floor.

Do you ever wonder how ice gets into the ice tray? When I go to get ice there is none in the tray. Don't you ever wonder how the ice ends up in the ice tray? I don't suppose you do.

I can't believe that people put the ice trays back in the refrigerator empty and that they are already eating and don't have to worry about it.

If I had a button off my pants, I would sew one on and not wait for someone else to do it.

Do you ever see me take the trash and crush it like that? No! You don't, It takes up more space in the trash container when you do that.

Don't pat yourself on the back, you are volunteering just so I can say thank you, forget it.

Get away and leave me alone for God's sake. God is going to punish you.

Is it that you are bored with nothing going on in your head that makes you feel that you have to pester me?

Tend to your business and leave my business alone, you don't want to help anyway; you just want to be a nuisance.

We can do this! We can do that! Don't be we-ing me.

When you start brushing my hair then you can determine how it looks. I like mine the way it is. It's my hair not yours.

You are always up to something, usually it's no good.

I don't know what goes on in that head of yours, you are evil. Just stay were you are and don't touch me.

I asked you a question and you answered with another question, the answer is, "I don't think so."

No, I don't like compliments from you, you say the same thing over and over.

All of your compliments are about my chest.

Were you raised in a barn, you have the manners of a pig.

There was an article in today's paper about maturity, it stated: Maturity does not come with age. You are an old man and I don't think you will ever mature. You are silly, a silly old man.

Talk, talk, talk and say nothing. that is, nothing worthwhile.

Wait a minute I will give you something to wipe your hand on so that you will not use fifteen paper towels from the paper rack. I try to conserve whenever possible.

When I die, you can find a young girl and all that they want is your money. You don't have anything else that is worth anything.

Everything else that you have is so old, that no one in her right mind would want it.

I am going to have you committed because you are a simpleton, a sicko.

I don't want you to buy me a five million dollar house; you would just fill it with crap like this one.

You don't do anything for me; you just want me to do something for you.

The cabinet door is open. No! It was not a fairy that left it open, you did.

I don't know why I blame you, I should have know by now that you never do anything the right way.

Don't you think I understood you the first time that you told me that?

You get up in the morning and don't have a clue which end is up.

I don't like or understand people who constantly talk about themselves and want all the praise in the world. Pat yourself on the back.

Good morning, and what in the hell is your problem?

Did you get up on the wrong side of the bed?

If you have something to say that is important, which I doubt, say it aloud and don't mumble under your breath.

What difference does it make to you how I feel, you don't give a penny, do you?

You criticize constantly but you don't do anything about it, you just criticize.

I am sick and tired of you with that, I should get a job shit.

I am retired and so are you. That damn pottery shop is not a workplace and you have no job. You are not the CEO of anything.

I don't understand how you can say that you are the CEO of a company when you are the only employee.

What you need is another job away from the house, and then I could have some peace.

Stay in your office or your nasty shop and mind your own business.

Leave me alone because you don't know how to do anything but pick on me.

Keep your mouth shut; every time you open it, something stupid comes out.

That is not a smart aleck remark, it is true you only love yourself.

Why do you want me to open the junk mail, I am the designated junk mail opener.

Here is something that you should open; it is an advertisement for a hearing aid.

You equate a wife with a child or servant, we wives have minds of our own and you, my friend, are up a creek without a paddle.

I know that I am sick, anyone who hangs around you as long as I have has to be sick.

You are someone who is always in need of help. I don't need any help, especially from you.

Unless I am talking about something that involves you, you never pay attention to what I am saying.

I don't understand why you always ask me "Why?"

I don't have to have a reason for not wanting to do something?

Would you please stop asking me why I don't want to do it.

Every time you take your pills in the morning, you spill them on the floor. Why don't you put them on the table instead of your warped hands?

I have told you a thousand times to pour your pills on a sheet of paper and not in your hands that is the reason you drop them. Try to do something right for a change.

I live with a man who has no concern for anyone but himself.

There should have been some way like it is done in Star Trek, so that we could have seen how each of us would be in the future. I am sure that we would have made other choices. I get on your nerves and you definitely get on my nerves.

You only have one expression on your face, "stupid."

You are just no good with modern gadgets. Don't put anything in your hands that is not antique, modern things you don't seem to understand and you destroy them.

You have nothing to do so you come looking for me. I am busy, so get out of here and stop meddling with me, find something to do.

Do I have to remind you of everything that needs to be done around this house?

What do you want now; I don't have time for you or to help you do anything.

I can't stand someone who takes on a task knowing full well that they can't do it by themselves.

Do you know what a dishwasher does? It washes the dishes and it can't wash them if you put them in the sink, can it?

Isn't it wonderful to know so much about everything? To be so smart about everything.

You don't make anything a possibility, with you everything that comes out of your mouth is a fact and the gospel truth. I know how intelligent you are; your intelligence told you that you were intelligent, you know everything. You have warm hands and you have a cold heart, haven't you heard that expression. Don't try thinking of something smart to say, it is too much work for you.

You have all these facts that come out of you head as if it is all true. Think about it, you state something and swear it is a fact when it is really not.

You head is to full of crap to allow you to think fast.

Who else would live with you? Ask yourself that question?

Why did you say that, you are saying that just to get me angry, and you succeeded? Get out of here and leave me alone.

Why do you follow me, I go in the living room and you come in there, I go to the bedroom and you come in there. I go in the kitchen and you come in there. You follow me around like a lap dog, get a life.

I'm pissed because when I walked in the door, no good morning. There was no how do you feel.

No! Did you mail my packages? Why do you think I went out, dumb bell?

I live with a computer and sometimes I think that the hard drive is broken or not operating properly.

The easiest thing to do is to put the top on a container when you open it and put it back when you finish with it. No one in this house knows how to do it. Yes, you are no one.

You have a very nasty mean streak, what do I call it, "passive aggression."

If you have nothing to say, say nothing, or keep your trap shut.

Do I have to remind you of everything that needs to be done around this house?

There is a twist to the song, "Jesus Loves Me." Here is how it goes, "Jesus Loves Nice People."

Look at you, you are putting tobacco in your pipe like you pee in the bowl, looking all over the place and not watching what you are doing. That is why you get tobacco all over your desk and the floor.

What do you think; you are a mind reader, if so you are getting the wrong message. Put that in that stupid pipe of yours and try smoking it.

You thought, you thought, well at least that is new.

I come home and you are sleeping in the chair. I quietly go in the spare room and make the bed, and then I quietly go in the kitchen and load the dishwasher.

I go into our bedroom and quietly fold some clothes. What I do not do is come in and yell, " Husband where are you?"

Why can't you do the same thing when you come in and I am resting?

I never wake you up when I come in, yet, you always wake me up with lots of noise.

Why do you always call me by name when there is no one here but the two of us in this house?

You can be a real smart aleck without even trying, get a grip on yourself. It really gets lonely in the house with no one to hold a conversation with.

I can't believe that I married a man with your genes, brains and character.

Your brains seem to shrink with age.

I think there is something inherently evil in some one who is constantly picking and teasing. You are one evil person.

If you were wrong some of the time, I would not have to always be right, Mr. know it all.

Now isn't that wonderful, you went into the cabinet, How do I know, you left it open? If you open something then close it, is that so difficult?

You always get bent out of shape about things that are not important, you just can't let things go. You Watfords are all mean and you are the meanest of the lot.

I can't believe that I married someone like you. I don't know what I was thinking.

No! I didn't think that I could change you after I married you, you are impossible.

You are like a damn child, someone has to follow behind you and correct the mistakes that you make.

I think you would die of boredom if you did not have me to pick on.

So we missed the party. I really don't know why anyone would tell you anything or invite you anyplace because you can't remember shit.

It's your back ache and I am thinking about you, not me, as usual you are thinking only of yourself.

Are you trying to be funny, well you are not.

You complain about the way people do things all the time, you always criticize and it's none of your business.

Go away; you are disturbing my peace of mind.

Do you realize that you give me a reason to fuss; now you come up with your stupid remarks?

I am sick of you asking me stupid questions, you sound like a child and no, I did not miss you.

Can't I sit and rest without you picking at me?

Look where you were sitting on the couch, there is a smudge from your pipe, you damn dirty man.

You just don't understand how to close cabinets at all, you are a real pain.

One day you might have to wait on me, but I can do this myself, save it for that day.

Clumsy, you are clumsy about everything that you do, including things that you don't do.

What's wrong again?" Do you see how boring you are. "What's wrong, what's wrong?"

I am tired of your junk all over the place, you are sorry, you are sorry, that is all I hear from you.

Give me a break. You didn't have anything when I met you, and you don't have a lot now.

No, I don't want to play that wife shit, today, tomorrow or ever.

You come up with wife; I am not a wife to you but someone who waits on you and someone that you want to nail.

Did you close the drawer? How can you open something and leave it like that. When you open it, you shut it.

Are you finished with the light, you could turn it out, you know. I was not the one that turned it on. If I had turned it on, I would have turned it off.

You are so infantile, why don't you act your age, you old coot.

Do it yourself, why do you always ask me to do things; You come in here and ask me to do something that you should do yourself.

Any statement that I make and you don't agree with is a fussing statement.

Just because it does not agree with your philosophy, it is fussing. You are a very sick man in both mind and body.

Is that cloth something that you are going to use to wash that shelf? That is my dishcloth, the rags are on the bottom shelf. I can't believe you, you pick up the first cloth that you see to wash that dirty shelf. Do you live here? Don't you know where anything is?

You should know better than to say that to me, "Don't forget it," Now you can do it yourself.

On Shopping

And much as Wine has play'd the Infidel,
And robb'd me of my Robe of Honour-Well
I often wonder what the Vintners buy
One half so precious as the Goods they sell.

Rubaiyat of Omar Khayyam

I am not going to buy anymore of that. It would have lasted me for two weeks and you eat it all in two days.

You are going to buy it yourself so that you can eat it all, like a pig.

I did not make a list and I really don't want you shopping with me. I am paying for the food and I will shop alone and purchase what I want to purchase.

You can come with me if you like but keep your trap shut and don't ask me why I am purchasing something.

I really don't want you shopping with me, I prefer to do it alone without you meddling.

You don't want to go to the super market with me because I don't have a list, then; I will take you home and go by myself. I have a list in my head.

So I use the Columbus system {Find something and land on it} when I type or shop for food, It gets the job done.

Why do you think that I do all the shopping, you would never buy anything that cost more than a quarter, you cheap bastard.

Why are you looking over my shoulder while I shop for food you are not paying for it, if you were, it would make no difference?

I can't believe that I am constantly being asked, what are you buying, what is that, do we need that?

Men should stay at home when their wives are grocery shopping and that means you.

Go sit in the car while I finish shopping and quit bothering me, unless you want to pay for the food.

There you go, headed for the car, because the thought of paying for the food is too much for you, you cheap jerk.

You went to the store and did not buy what I asked for. No! you did not, where is the ice cream?

Oh, so you forgot, so what else is new?

Look at the milk that you brought at the store, it is buttermilk.

Don't you ever look at what you are buying, no, you just look at the price and purchase the cheapest one that you can find.

You are so cheap you looked at the price and purchased the cheapest milk that you could find.

I ask you to purchase a single item at the grocery store; I wanted milk, regular milk not buttermilk. Do you expect me to use buttermilk? I don't know of a single person that drinks buttermilk or uses buttermilk.

I don't drink buttermilk. Why don't you try drinking it? You are the one that made the purchase.

I do not care why they sell it, I don't want it.

Do you expect me to use buttermilk on my cereal? That is the last time that I will ever ask you to purchase anything at the store, you cheap jerk.

I still can't understand what is wrong with a man that makes it impossible to purchase the right milk, are men really that dumb?

What is wrong with a man's ability that he can't chose the right milk.

How many times do I have to tell you that I don't like buttermilk? What in the hell is buttermilk anyway?

No! I don't want you to buy the milk, you always look for the cheapest brand and then you buy it.

You take the buttermilk back if you want too; you are the one who purchased it.

You can eat it if you like or go purchase some more buttermilk for your cheap self.

You can't be trusted to make a purchase at the store, you are too obsessed with the price and will not purchase anything that costs more than ninety nine cents.

I don't understand people like you, you didn't buy it but and you call it ugly.

You are a piece of work. If you can't say something nice, don't say anything at all and that is universal.

You expect me to pull things out of the hat. I told you that I left my credit cards at home and I could only buy food. Yet you expect me to buy Raid, Drano and everything else.

I am going grocery shopping alone and I have a list of what I want as if that is any of your business.

If the list is in my head what difference does it make, I buy the groceries with my money.

Yes, I am going shopping but I am not going all over the world looking for something that you want. If you want something at the store go and get it yourself.

You can drive, not really well, but enough to go the store for yourself.

What you want is at Wal-Mart and I don't shop there. I don't care what their prices are, I am not going to that junky place for you or anyone else.

Just Talking

And strange to tell, among this Earthen Lot
Some could articulate, while others not:
And suddenly one more impatient cried-
"Who is the Potter, pray, and who the pot?"

Rubaiyat of Omar Khayyam.

My mother did not teach me to make smart remarks; I learned that on my own.

You don't have the humor to make smart remarks; humor is something that you do not possess.

Scotty, would you please take the time to beam me up, there is not one form of intelligent life down here.

Life is filled with surprises and you, my man, are the biggest one in my life! {Figure that one out}

You always take what people say too seriously, stop and smell the roses.

You are not important enough for anyone to be discussing.

I think I will talk to you while you are trying to read as you do me. Let's have a conversation about nothing.

Who are you talking to, what are you eating, and what are you watching on television? Is any of that any of your business?

If you have said that once, you have said it ten thousand times or more.

You seem to think that what I say is funny or a joke, especially about your bad habits. Anyway, you just ignore whatever I say.

Why do you have to call the pills pain killers, no one but you calls them pain killers. They don't kill pain.

I was at the Department of Motor Vehicles today and I said to the girl behind the window. "I have insurance on my camper, do I need papers to prove it."

She said, "You mean <u>in</u>surance."

I said quietly to that southern bitch, "No, I mean in<u>sur</u>ance, if you check the dictionary you will see that the accent is not above the "<u>in</u>" but above the "<u>sur</u>."

That is the last time that she will try to correct a little old black lady.

You say that but you don't believe it, you can't change the past, it is over. Can't you forget it, the past, that is?

That is typical of you, it is a wonder that you are not finishing the conversation that we started last week.

I would not do anything for you if someone paid me a thousand dollars, do something for yourself. What do you do for me?

I don't mean that, you do that for yourself not for me. If you think you are doing it for me just quit.

Yes, Howard Cosell is dead and you should know that, you watch sports sometimes but then you are dead also.

Same old thing, I am talking about one thing and you don't even acknowledge what I am talking about and then you bring up an entirely different topic.

Yes, you make life interesting, but I could get along very well without all this adventure in my life.

What is it in that big head of yours that makes you think that you know what I want?

I know what I want and it is not what you want to give me.

I think you feel guilty when you are not doing something, I don't, I am just going to sit here and watch golf. That is something that I could not do when I was younger.

Rock three times "Old man," and on the third time, you should be able to get out of that chair.

Women don't have to do everything around the house, some of the things you men could do. You could make the call for the potluck dinner and explain what we are bringing or is that too much to ask of a man?

I don't know why you can't fill that small space between your ears with something worth talking about.

What do you mean "We", you and that "We" stuff has to stop.

I can be talking about something and you just change the subject to something else. You never pay attention to what I am talking about. You mind is always on something else.

I did not say that people who talk to themselves are crazy. You are always talking to yourself. Maybe you are a little bit crazy, considering the way you carry on a conversation with yourself.

I am not jealous because I have no one to talk to. I don't need anyone to talk to when I am alone.

Why do you need someone to talk to when you are by yourself?

There is no need for you to ignore me when I am talking to you but you do it anyway.

No, you were not thinking, nor do you have a lot to think with.

By the way did you like my orange sherbet, how do I know that you ate it. You left the bowl out. If you cleaned up after yourself, no one would ever know what you do.

Yes, and why does it rain on Tuesday?

You came in here with that lie, "Look what I brought you." You don't do things like that, you are not that thoughtful. I knew you had won it in some raffle or found it on the side of the road. Now you tell me you won it in a raffle, but I already knew that.

Are your arms long enough, then, just pat your self on the back.

Sit in your chair because if you got up to do something for yourself, you would break into two pieces.

I don't sit here and say, husband, husband, and husband as if there is no one else in this room but the two of us.

Yes, I will cut your hair but I want to save it to clean my pots with it.

You want me to cut your hair only because you are too cheap to pay the barber to do it.

Do you ever know when you are being ignored.

I know what you are saying, and the dog ate my homework too.

You like Beethoven because you can't hear well and his music is just loud, you have no music ability and you sing off key.

When we are in church please do not sing, you are so far off key that it disturbs my singing. Just move you mouth and pretend to be singing. Every one in the congregation will appreciate not hearing you.

The flowers are lovely, thank you, how many times do I have to say that? Do you ever do anything that you don't have to be praised for?

Thank you is all that you are going to get, flowers or no flowers.

The look on your face is pure pleasure, it says now I have aggravated her and I am happy.

I just finished telling you that and I am not going to tell you again what is wrong with me.

No! It is "no thank you", saying no is rude.

You don't think that was rude, instead of saying, no thank you, just no?

How do you know that? Oh, I forget, you know everything.

You can't lie with a straight face. That has always gotten you in trouble.

You don't know what wishy-washy means; it means you don't have decision-making qualities.

Nothing in the world is worse than a person who is wishy-washy and can't make up their mind about something.

You spell wishy-washy, I don't spell words for that dumb book and that shit that you are always writing down.

You do things just to annoy me, grow up.

You should say, "Thank you Madam" because you sound like a child.

You just like blond women, it has nothing to do with what V.J. Sing said about Anika.

If you got married again, it would be a really ugly woman, only an ugly woman would put up with your shit.

Are you hard of hearing? I think you are hard of hearing or you have selective hearing.

I am not listening to you, don't you know that? I am not the least bit interested in what you have to say; I know it is going to be about sex anyway.

I ask you for help and all you can do is criticize. You are a piece of work.

You should really have your ears checked and get a good hearing aid.

Don't you think easing into that chair would be better. You are going to end up on the floor.

Why do you flop in the chair like that? The springs in the chair can't take it. You are going to break the chair.

Do you want an ash tray rather than use the table for your ashes.

You want to be thanked for everything that you do, even when it is not done properly.

Everything that you are involved in, and it is a lot, you expect me to be enthusiastic about as you are.

Can't you understand that I am not interested in your projects. I don't like the people that attend your pottery shows, the people who attend are all phonies.

You are the bumblest person in the world, you just bumble your way through life and anything that you do.

When are you going to realize that you are not special and that the world does not revolve around you.

Can't you think of something smart to say. I don't suppose you have the brains for it.

Your words always come back to you because you talk crazy talk. Your conversational skills are very limited and most of the time none existent.

It is just your way of annoying me, get a life.

You use the word "dance" with what you do, you don't "dance."

I don't believe you, you can't get anything straight.

I heard you, that was witty, quite uncharacteristic for you, you are never witty.

Can't you talk to me without putting your hands all over me.

You are giving me credit and not taking it yourself, is that refreshing or what?

You are a growing boy all right, the only problem is that you are not built like one.

Don't you think that you should have your ears cleaned out, you would not always be asking, " What did she say?", "What did he say?"

Get off your soap box fella, you get all bent out of shape over other people's problems.

"What did I do?" "What did I do?" Don't I sound like you?

You have your computer so loud that the neighbors across the street can hear it.

If you picked up your feet, you would not slip on things.

Why do you sit and dream up crazy stuff.

I didn't like skiing when I was young and I have no intentions of doing it now.

No, I would not marry you again or marry any other member of the male population.

This expecting to be waited upon is enough to drive one to drink.

You don't have to act like an old man. You should just act like a mature man.

Someone lied to you and told you that you knew what you were talking about.

Are you going to buy her a franchise to manufacture General Motors cars, I don't think so?

You are still letting people use your head.

Why do you do that? Forget about what has happened in the past. It's not like you can change it. It is gone so just forget it, if you can.

Anyway, it is not important in the scheme of things.

Most elevators go to the top floor. I think your elevator stopped at the second floor.

Being nice is asking, "How do you feel?" and doing kind things.

You could start by taking charge of your own head, thinking and doing for yourself.

Why do you stand like that, you look like a blessed ape.

As you have stated many times, "marriage is a funeral where one smells his own flowers."

Why do you have to get credit for the least little thing that you do?

Do you want to put a tape recorder on so that you will not have to repeat the same thing over and over?

I don't worry about what happened an hour or two hours ago because it makes no difference and I can't change what has happened.

You have to learn to do the same thing.

When our daughter Barbra moved to California, she ask the lady next door about the weather, the lady answered, "every day same".

That is just the way you are, like a walking tape recorder, everyday the same.

The same joke, the same clothes, the same question, "Every day the same."

Why don't you stop saying, "That is what I am talking about?" You are not talking about anything and it sounds stupid.

The very fact that I live with you is all the loving that you deserve.

What are you doing? What are you breathing,? Where are you going? What are you thinking? This is what I have to put up with.

You continuously repeat yourself that is what all old people do.

If you did not always drop things, you would not have the problem of picking them up.

I have never seen a monument made for one who brags.

The only reason we are still together after fifty-four years is because you are too old and bent over to find someone else and I don't want anyone else.

Don't you ever get tired of meddling with me, what are you doing? Who is on the phone? What are you eating? Damn, there is no privacy around here.

You are so superficial, you really are, everything that you do is annoying.

You want to know if I am alive, why do you have to know my every move. I am going to shit, do you care.

It's the broken record that I am talking about, that is the third time you have said that. You have a bad case of CRS.

{Can't remember shit}

Why can't you just answer a simple question without making some dumb remark completely off the topic.

I am discussing a topic and you come up with something out of left field.

The problem is that you can't remember what you say and you always repeat yourself.

It is odd to me that you are so excessive, you always have to have a lot of everything.

Excuse me! Are you putting me down, yes, you are, or are you just trying to be funny?

I want you to start looking at me as a person and not as a slave or someone whose role in life is just to wait on you hand and foot.

The next time I am sick I am going to throw up on you so that you will see that I am really sick.

You have proved something that I have said all along, you are passive aggressive. You have a mean streak.

Are you going back out today, you still have your hat on, take it off please.

Every time I look at you, you say, "What's wrong".

You are going to get on my nerves today. I see that right now.

I am sick and I can always depend upon you for sympathy, it exudes from your body.

If someone is sick, that is too bad.

No! today is not the sixteenth, it's your birthday, were you born on the sixteenth, no you were born on the fourth of July?

I have to go in your office and clean up your mess before the house cleaners get here.

Why? You would never understand with your small mind so forget it.

I explained why I want your office neat and clean before she comes. I don't want anyone to think that I live in a pigsty.

You don't have any feelings and it is because you never learned any when you were growing up.

You are insensitive, there isn't a sensitive bone in that body of yours.

You are a big phony, whenever you give a compliment it is for yourself.

You didn't grow up, you just got older but never matured. Oh! for God's sake, you will sit on anything, you just come in and sit down, damn.

Yes, you are like that, once you have made up your mind about something you can never change.

I spend too much time cleaning up after you, you should not be so messy.

Your hair on top of your head is dark because there is very little of it and your scalp is showing through.

There I was trying to share and you take the whole thing, all that you think of is me, me and more me.

Why? WHY? Why? That is all that I hear from you. Why are you doing this, what are you doing that, Jesus?

Are you doing that, just to aggravate me? Those are the things that I don't like and you know it.

You always have to change something, just have to put your hands on it, don't you?

If you want to talk to me, don't ask stupid questions, do I know the name of your company?

I have lived with you for fifty years and you still ask me dumb questions.

You comes first, second, and third and I might be a distant fourth.

You have a habit that really annoys me, you can never make up your mind.

You always call, wife, wife, wife is there anyone else in this room besides you and me?

There in no one else in this room unless you are talking to yourself as you usually do.

You can't stay home and do nothing. I can stay home and do nothing and it doesn't bother me. I can just sit and watch television and be happy.

Your television is on in your room why are you coming in here?

No matter where I go you have to come.

I feel like I have Velcro attached to me.

Ask you a question and you always have to think about it.

You always come out with something stupid.

You are really a piece of work.

I am talking about someone else, don't put yourself in it. It has nothing to do with you.

Go to bed early tonight, we bowl tomorrow, remember you are not as young as you used to be.

You are the coldest person in the entire world.

You are back from your trip and back into the same old routine, lazy and wanting to be waited on, forget it.

Do I have to remind you of everything that needs to be done around this house?

Why do you constantly want to be stroked, you can look and see what is nice about you without asking someone about it.

I don't sit here and say, husband, husband, husband as if there is no one else in the room but the two of us. You sound like you are in a hog-calling contest.

You are like some people I know, they never grow up and become adults.

Yes, I do have a job and there are no rewards, my job is living with a dimwit.

I am retired and I don't need a job. You are not the CEO of any company.

Do you want to go and hang up that other phone before you forget it.

You know what is on my mind, you know everything you are, a Watford.

Definitely don't say that again. What is done is done, it is another day.

Find something that will give you pleasure other than picking and following me around the house.

Yes, everything goes away eventually, it's called death.

You are not a creature of habit, you are just boring.

I have a little shadow that goes in and out with me and what can be the use of him I cannot see.

Did you have a Christmas tree when you were a child, that is all that I asked, I didn't ask what was under it?

If there were food under it would have been gone in a minute.

I don't know why you figure things, you figure this, you figure that. You are always figuring something.

You are "sorry" is an empty "sorry", You say "sorry" like kids say "sorry", it just means get off my back.

I don't know whether that is being passive aggressive or what, you always ask and you know that I don't want to go.

Our conversation is so boring, the value of *Pi* and the millionth digit in the pi series. Who in the hell cares about such stuff. you might be interested in the millionth digit of pi but I am not.

I am not interested in the millionth digit of Pi. Does the value of Pi help me breath, does it help me walk, does it do any damn thing for me, no, so just forget it if that is all you have to talk about.

I am not interested in that crap that you have in that brain of yours.

If you want to hear Shakespeare on our trip you had better drive your own car. I am not interested in that crap, I have a mystery that we are going to listen too.

You didn't put the corn beef back in the refrigerator the way I put it back, so that is how I know that you ate some of it.

Be quiet I can't hear what is going on with all your talking.

When are you going to grow up and forget what happened to you in your childhood.

Do you ever do anything for yourself; you just sit and ask other people to do it? That is very annoying.

Now, how difficult was that, why didn't you call the security gate, you could have done it as I did, no you have to have someone do it for you, you are a trip?

Where did you get that mean streak, here I am minding my own business and you come in here just to disturb me, that is being mean?

You always put the top light on and is not as bright as the side light, why do you do that?

You are not going to grow up ever, so, forget it.

How many times are you going to read that note from your daughter about your book, you are weird..

You should forget all those negative things you hold in your head and you would live longer.

It is none of your business, You have a horrible, horrible way of behaving and it is passive aggressive.

You are a pain in the ass, I get tired of this come here, come here, come here.

If it is not about you it isn't about anyone, you have a bad habit of thinking of no one but yourself.

Why do you want to come in here and disturb me?

I am not interested in anything that you have to say because it has no substance.

If it's not about you, it is not about anything.

No! I don't want to go to New York City to see the gates in Central Park. What is the point of traveling all that way there to see those flags waving?

It is like someone saying I want to see a dead person.

If I lived in New York City I would not go out of my way to see those flags.

You look a little low today, are you feeling OK. Don't give me that look and don't come up with something stupid.

Don't start that, you are a constant pain in the neck.

Don't creep up on me looking like you look.

It would frighten you or anyone else if they turned around and saw a big black bear in their view, don't come up on me like that.

It is no wonder you don't want me to go and visit our daughter. I am your damn housekeeper and your finder and someone to nail.

You always repeat yourself? Do you think that by repeating something it will change? If you say it one thousand times it will still be the same.

Where am I, what are you doing, where are you going, what are you drinking? I get fed up with your questions, get out of here and leave me alone.

I can't take it, will you please stop asking me. What are you doing, where are you going, what are you eating, its enough to drive a person crazy?

You should go out and buy some lotion, use what I have or forget it.

Act like an intelligent human being, I get really tired of the way that you act.

Why do you repeat yourself, one time should be enough.

Do you notice how everything reverts back to you, no matter what we are talking about? I guess you can't help it.

Because it snows on Tuesday - Why do you ask stupid questions when I am in here minding my own business.

Does it say stupid written across my forehead?

What would you do if I were not around; honestly, there is no one in the world that would do the things that you ask me to do?

That is what is wrong with you, you never let the little child out, he is still inside of you with that old man.

That is really why I don't ask you anything, you always come up with something silly.

Don't tell me that again, I am tired of hearing it. I am proud of you but enough is enough, "Bless Bess!"

Why do you want to disturb me when I am comfortable, you just stay over there where you are.

You are full of the devil, you do that just to get on my nerves, you really have a mean streak.

Why didn't you smile when we took our church pictures, you sat there looking like death warmed over?

It's no wonder the man didn't insist that you buy them or try to sell them to us.

You didn't smile and you looked like Frankenstein's monster.

You have a nice face but it is always screwed up.

I would rather do it myself than to have you think that I don't know what I'm doing.

Why do you blow up like that, you send me to do the dirty work, like taking something back to the store and then question how I do it? You had better learn to control yourself and run you own errands.

You tend to put all women in the same category with your one track mind.

Don't say that you are doing it for me, you are doing it for yourself.

If you do anything it is for yourself.

You have your say and then other people have to shut up, forget it, I will have my say also.

Get off your soapbox fella, you get all bent out of shape over other people's problems.

I did not say anything about your half closed eyes.

If that is your way of annoying me, it did not work, try something else.

All those people out there who think you are so great, that you are really a good person, they don't have to live with you.

You don't see anything wrong with the way you think and behave.

I am talking about myself and all of a sudden it's about you.

You are absolutely crude.

No verbal skills at all, you should learn to carry on a normal conversation. I mean a conversation that does not involve sex.

Your reasoning doesn't sound right.

You just don't have a sense of humor.

When someone says they don't like something why must you insist that they have it?

I don't want to get nailed and I don't mean maybe!

Sure you will do anything that I want you to do and then talk about it.

What are you going to do? just go into your dirty pottery shop, I want to sit in here by myself.

Why don't you stop? That is very annoying but then you know that.

You carry too much baggage in your head from insulting remarks that people say to you. I am not going to let people have rent free space in my head. You would be a happier person if you let things go.

Don't you ever stay on a subject? You are impossible. I really don't know why I try, talking to you is like talking to a six year old or a brick shit house.

I was going to try to talk to you about your vertigo, forget it.

Your maturity stopped at fourteen about the time when you discovered sex.

In a few minutes you will ask me what I said. I would not have to repeat myself if you listen once and awhile. Getting a hearing aid might help also.

No, I don't want to talk to you because you have nothing to say. You have had nothing to say for the past twenty years at least nothing that is worth listening too.

Talking to you is like having a one way conversation with one's self.

You can't hear anything that I say and you can't remember where you have been if you went there yesterday.

You keep your head too full of unnecessary information, like all those poems that you remember.

Sometimes I think that life just passes you by and goes on it's merry way without you.

Your head stays where it stays and I don't feel like talking to you.

Can't we have anytime together without you talking about sex?

That seems like your goal in life to be a pain in the ass. Get a life.

What did you say? If you say it under your breath it is usually nothing worth hearing.

You just talk about shit all the time, you don't have a conversation about anything normal, it is a nuisance. You are a Watford and Watfords do evil things, Watfords don't think beyond evil.

I am ignoring you, don't you understand what it is like to be ignored, jeez.

You should give me two weeks of rest from your verbiage or maybe two years.

I feel like making you repeat what I just said, you know that you were not paying attention and haven't a clue as to what I was talking about.

Who Is The Boss

> I don't want to spend any quality time with you and I definitely don't want to get nailed.

Oh, come with old Khayyam, and leave the Wise
To talk; one thing is certain, that Life flies;
One thing is certain, and the Rest is Lies;
The Flower that once has blown for ever dies.

Rubaiyat of Omar Khayyam

I am minding my business, what are you doing minding my business also.

You really try to boss me around and the word is "try".

I am an old woman and you are an old man and don't forget it.

When you say "We" are doing this and "we" are doing that" it is a disservice and I don't know who the "we" is that you are talking about.

Now you are going to tell me how to talk and how to think, forget it.

You make a decision and expect me to go along with it, I will not. You can do what you want to and I will do the same, remember that.

I don't need you to tell me how to lose weight, you fat old man.

Are you going to take responsibility for that, I don't think so.

It is ours only if I say it is ours?

You don't have a wife, you screwed up, it doesn't work that way. I don't dress for you. I dress for me.

You come in here with you belt below your belly and want me to dress up. I don't dress up for a clown.

You are always coming up with "We" are going to this and "we" are going to do that." Who is this "we" you are talking about.

Please don't use "we" when referring to us, there is no "We" here. There is just you and me. It is we only when you want me to do something stupid and disgusting.

Somehow in your head you think that you should be waited upon, you can forget that.

You are going to tell me what I am going to do first, you can forget it.

Every chance you get you come over to kiss me. That is used as a weapon by you, it is like saying, "I am in control." You are in control of nothing.

You make a decision and expect me to go along with it. No!, I will not.

You are too accustomed to having people wait on you. You can do this, you can do that, forget it.

You are not disabled, so do things for yourself.

I just tapped you and that does not call for a police report.

You would not have a reason to hit me because I am not going to be feeling all over your body and if you did you would end up dead.

Your daughter picked a husband just like you. Very difficult to live with, well, you used to be that way, you have mellowed out in your old age.

Three of them picked husbands that they can control not much like you. You have to have your way, but not in this house.

I am surprised that you think you have some kind of control. The only one that you have control over is yourself except when you have to pee.

I never said "obey" you tend to take those vows too seriously.

What is this "obey" shit anyway.

There was no obey part of our marriage vows and if there were it was a joke.

I will never obey anyone who is my equal.

I don't obey anyone.

I don't care what other husbands do or don't do.

I will only obey my father and mother, do you get that?

Come off that "We stuff". I have planned my day.

You still don't hear what I am saying, go by yourself. I am not going anyplace with you. Yea, he got it!

You think that because you are the male in this house you should be waited on. Well you have another thought coming.

For the umpteenth time I don't want to play wife, any way it would mean that I have a husband.

What is this "we" ? You always come up with this "we" stuff. There is no "we" there is just you and me and if you want to do something, do it by yourself.

We! will not be going with you. You put yourself in things and expect me to participate. That is your affair, you go.

I am not going with you.

You can forget about my going, because I am not.

You will not use my time, that is not the way I want to use my time.

I notice how you are telling me you are going to get me to do something.

Your opinion doesn't count with me, can't you see that?

I don't need your opinion on what I do or don't do.

You don't have anyone that you are paying to get anything. Anyway this is my body and it is not for sale.

Just understand that I am not the least bit interested in your activities.

I have my own activities and I don't expect you to be involved in them.

You don't tell anyone to do something, when is that going to dawn on you? Even the children are too old to be told what to do.

Men have the attitude that they will let you do something.

You are going to tell me how to cook something as if I need your advice on cooking.

I might look like the cooking lady on television but she doesn't have an ass hole standing over here and commenting.

The Kitchen is my domain, get out. Go to your pottery shop and do some work, Mr. CEO.

I don't want you doing it because I just don't like it. Keep your hands to yourself.

You want everything to run on your schedule, that is the way you are. Everything centers around you and what you want, that is not the way it is going to be.

You are going to let, let, let me do something.

You are just nosy, you have to know what I am doing, it is none of your business.

I still think old people should have hearing aids. That is if they want to hear anything. I don't think you want to hear what I have to say, that is why you have not obtained a hearing aid.

I don't need your sympathy it is so contrived.

You have to do this, you have to do that. I don't have to do anything - get it!

Don't "let's" be doing anything, you do your thing and I will do my thing.

You stated that, "At least I didn't have to cook dinner." Listen to yourself. I don't have to cook dinner or do anything else that I don't want to do.

Why are you watching my every move and commenting on what I am doing? It is none of your business.

When is it going to dawn on you that you can't make me do anything?

You are going to let me - sounds like you are giving me permission.

I am retired, I do what I want to, when I want too, and I don't do what I don't want too.

What is this let shit, when is it going to occur to you that you are not going to let me do something, forget it.

Who told you that you were in charge, those stupid people in Winton.

Why do you question everything that I say, if I say there is none, then there is none.

Somehow you think you are in charge, you are in charge of nothing.

You will do anything that I ask? Then go to hell.

I don't need permission to do anything.

You married the wrong woman, you should have married one of those country women from your home town,

The kind of woman that says yes sir and no sir.

Someone gave you the attitude that you are to be waited on that is not going to happen around here.

You don't have to answer, I don't give a shit if you answer or you don't.

Mind your business. There is nothing that I can do that you don't comment on. Mind your business.

Go away, you have nothing to do so you are going to pick on me. You had better get out of here.

Why does everything have to be about you, what you did, what you think, you are not that important to me, yourself or anyone else?

Get out, I swear you are so filled with yourself, get out of here.

Get a life!

Sometimes I wonder where your mind is.

You are not blind but you are going to be blind if you don't get out of here. That is your biggest problem you consider me a peon.

I don't have to do what you tell me to do. I have a brain and it works better than yours, which is in you pants.

Do what you want to do, you are so annoying, all you do is pick on me. Get out of here and leave me alone.

There are some people who are weak, I am not one of them.

I have learned to do things for myself, you should learn to do things for yourself too.

I know you grew up without heat in the house except a stove. When I get up, I am not going to make a fire. I am not going to be cold in this house and I am not going to try to make a fire in the fireplace.

You can make a fire if you want to. You are so cheap you are thinking of the cost of heating the damn house.

Who is stupid enough to live with you.

Are you talking or has your mind gone some place else.

That is the other thing, "come over here," I am sick and tired of being summoned like some damn dog, no please or thank you.

Don't sit over here by me, sit someplace else.

Tell me what's on my mind, Mr. mind reader.

You are giving me permission to do something, thanks for your support.

Keep telling yourself that and you will believe it.

You sound like a blooming idiot, like someone who has been in an asylum, and just wants to hear his own voice

Pinhead! we!, we!, can do this, we can do that, We, We, We.

Sometimes I wonder what my role in the house really is, it is always will you do this, will you do that.

You ask, "Can I come in and spend some quality time with you?"

"Hell no! You don't know what quality time is, all you want to do is annoy me.

Beam me up Scotty; there is no intelligent life down here.

If it has been two years for you, then it has been two years for me and you don't see me acting that way.

No!!!

Because it snows on Tuesday and it rains on Wednesday, why do you ask stupid questions? I am here minding my business and in you come with your stupid questions.

Why do you think your kisses have some sort of power? It is always do you want a kiss, kiss this, kiss that.

I am going to B.E.D. and the answer is no. It is not the 16th or the 2nd of the month so leave me alone. No! I don't feel well and I think I am not going to feel well the rest of the month and the rest of the year so you can forget any plans that you have.

You are not the boss around here, there is no boss in this house.

Why do you deserve honors for repairing something around the house, it is your job?

Yes, I changed the place where the bread stays just to confuse you. You will forever be going over there for the bread.

Why is that chair squeaking like that? I would have put oil on it a long time ago, keeping all that noise.

Why do you expect kudos for everything that you do? Just pat yourself on the back.

I purchased those tools for myself because you never know where yours are and now you want to use mine. Please put my tools back where they belong when you finish with them. So that when I want to use them, I will know where to find them.

You could have saved yourself a lot of work by doing that right in the first place.

You never finish anything, everything gets started but nothing is ever completed.

I am going to say this one last time, "Get some paint and paint the inside of the house and don't hire someone to do it for you.

I don't know why I say that I know what you are going to do.

You don't have a clue as to what is going on in this house. I purchased that item two months ago.

You don't do anything about anything but that pottery shop and you don't know what is going on in there.

Why don't you stop patting yourself on the back when you do something for the house.

You have to have someone validate everything that you do. Can't you do something without telling the world that you are doing it and expecting praise.

If you like what little you do around the house that should be enough.

I went out and turned the electricity to the heating unit off, someone had to do something and you would just sit there and work on your computer. Thanks for your help.

I know that you have a job, Mr. Potter, so that keeps you from doing things around the house and answering the phone. Your daughter, Becky, called twice today and you did not even answer the phone.

Get down off that ladder before you fall and break you leg or something else and it is not the something else that I am worried about. I don't want to visit you in the hospital and hear you talking about the big tit nurses.

You never do anything right around this house, you just do it.

When you are nailing a nail in a board you can't just put one nail it , you have to over do it and put in twenty nails.

That was the way my father did things and it drove my mother crazy; now I have a husband that does the same thing.

That is not why I married you, you are not like my father in many ways.

You are going to break that chair the way that you pounce in it, and you would never repair it if you broke it.

Why do I live with someone like you who can't do things the right way?

You do everything half ass.

I don't know how anyone who bumbles about like you, can exist in the world.

Sometimes I think you hear just what you want to hear. At any rate you don't hear me when I ask you to do something around the house.

Forget it, I don't do yard work, that is your job. Go out and hire someone to do it like you do everything else. I live in a pigsty in this house, nothing stays nice and tidy around here and you make no repairs until things fall apart.

I just can't leave you alone with gadgets of any type, you are no good when it comes to the gadgets around the house. When are you going to learn to program the VCR?

Take all that excess energy and do something around the house and you would be doing something worthwhile.

You sit in your chair because if you got up and tried to do something for yourself you would break your back.

You never do things the right way, you are awkward and in a hurry to get something done.

Why don't you plan what you are going to do and then start on a project?

You know what would look good to me, an empty garage can?

Everything that you do is half ass, with everything all mixed up. Think about it, do you have some system for doing things?

With you, everything has to be done yesterday, you never make plans for the projects that you start.

One of these days you will get tired of doing that and fix that light.

That light has been broken for ten years and you have never thought of fixing it.

You spilled ice cream and cake on the rug and made no attempt to clean it up, you slob. You would live in a pigpen.

I thought I would do this, I thought I would do that, you thought that you would do nothing as usual.

Why do you hold the soda can like that, it is always bent after you use it?

Hold the can like this with two hands and it will not bend, forget it, you are too awkward.

Basically, that is your motivation, you don't want anyone to think that you can't do something.

I don't really understand people who are such pessimists, this wouldn't work or that wouldn't work. You just don't want to make the repairs.

I would really like to see you do some work around her.

The walls in this house have not been painted in eighteen years, not since we moved here.

Now you are going out to hire someone to do the painting, you lazy man.

Look at this I live in a barn, the damn place is falling down around us.

This place is a mess with two grown people living here, clean up your mess.

Why can't you get around to fixing things in the house? I told you the light was out in the bathroom two weeks ago. Still you have not fixed it. I would do it my self if I knew how to get the cover off.

Please show me how you opened that light fixture. The next time it goes out, I will not have to wait for two weeks to have light in the bathroom working.

Do you realize that nothing gets fixed in this house until I tell you about it twenty times? All you think about is sex, pottery and your computer in that order.

You would not forget to do things around the house if you made repairs immediately when something goes wrong.

If your potter's wheel stopped working I don't think you would forget it. If that computer of yours stopped working, I don't think you would forget to repair it or have it done.

You would not forget if you went straight to the chore and got it done as soon as it needed fixing.

Your philosophy is, "Don't fix it and it will go away."

Television

And this I know; whether the one true light,
Kindle to Love, or Wrath consume me quite
One glimpse of It within the Tavern caught
Better than in the Temple lost outright.

Rubiayat of Omar Khayyam

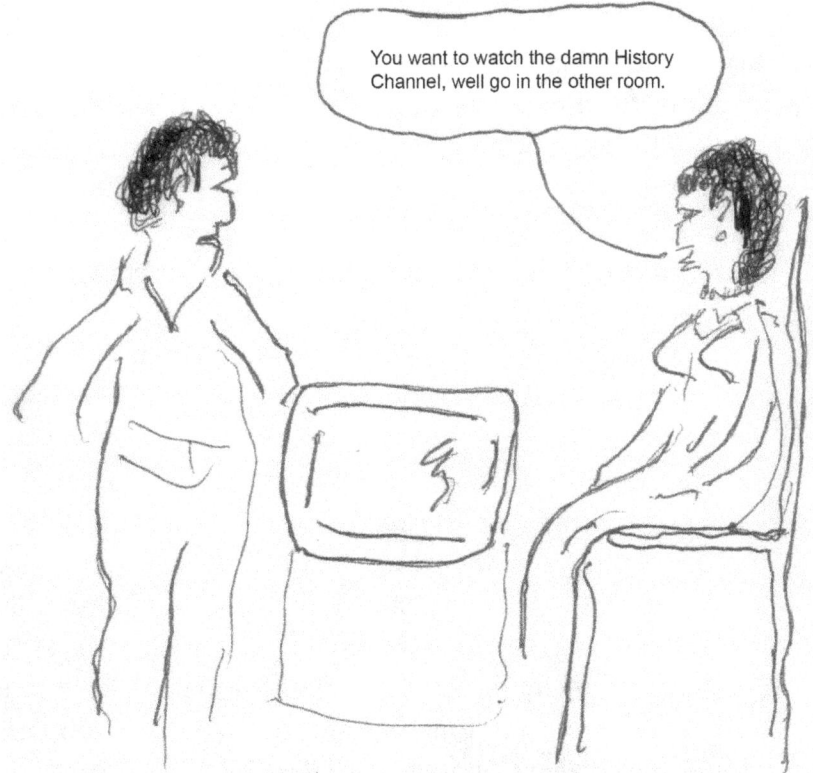

You have a very narrow vision. Get Star Trek or the History channel 24 hours a day. Why don't you find them?

All that you watch is Star Trek, you have a one track mind. If you want to watch Star Trek go in the study and watch it and leave me alone to watch what I want to watch.

What is the point in telling you anything about what I am looking at on television, all you watch is the History channel and Star Trek. There are other channels on television, did you not know that?

"We", don't have to watch the Tony awards - "We" can go in the other room and turn on that dumb History channel and look at it.

Don't come in here. I don't need someone sitting at the table watching me fix dinner, stay in there and continue watching that stupid History channel or is it Star Trek. Those are the only channel that you watch anyway?

Please don't stay in here and watch television with me, I don't feel like answering questions and telling you what is going on.

I am looking at television and I know what is going on. You can't follow the action, don't expect me to explain it to you.

They show scenes like that on television because they know that men and fools like you look at them.

That crap is not for women because women are too smart to be taken in by that stupid television.

So you want to watch the news, well, you know where to go.

I should block the History channel, then you would lose your mind.

Instead of looking for the television remote you just take the one in the kitchen that belongs to that television. Why can't you keep up with the remote that belongs to the television in your study.

If you want to watch television, go in the other room and turn on the only channel that you know.

You had better laugh because that is all the pleasure that you are going to get.

You should not watch television, you can't keep up with what is going on. That is why you always watch one channel, the History channel.

How much pleasure does it give you to talk to the television set? That man is making millions and you call him a stupid ass. Yet you are sitting here making nothing.

I slam the television station changer down because it does not belong in that room, there is a special place for it and it belongs in here. In an hour or so you will be asking me where it is located. Yes, I watched that Netflix movie by myself and I was saying to myself, " I am glad that my husband is not here, he would be asking me to interpret what was being said."

I don't understand why you watch only the History channel. It is the same thing day to day, war and more war, and it is boring.

What's going on? You can't follow the plot and I am tired of explaining it to you.

I am sitting down with a movie in one hand and the remote in the other, what else do you want to know.

No, you can't carry me like the guy on television is carrying that woman. In the first pace you are too bent over and arthritic and in the second place, I am too fat. You can forget it.

Thank you, is that some TV commercial that you have been watching and saying to me all day.

Thank you, hell, you need to thank someone for putting up with you.

I look at what I want to look at on the television, not what you want to look at.

I am watching television and you come in and start talking. I miss everything that is going on and then you have the nerve to ask me what is happening on the show.

No! I don't want a kiss, would you leave me alone. Why do you pick on me like that as soon as you see me watching television.

All you ever want to watch is Star Trek or the History channel and you have no idea when they come on. Stop asking me when it comes on because I don't watch it and I am not interested in when it comes on or what channel.

Why do you come in and want me to change the channel. I am the one looking at this television, you are a nuisance.

Stop asking me about it, I am not interested in that stupid show. No, I don't want to watch the History channel, it is just some stupid war. It's just a show put on by some stupid people and there is nothing that I can do about it.

Go to another television if you want to see what's going on in that dumb war.

Don't watch this if you can't follow the story and want me to explain it to you. Go back to your study and watch the History channel since that is the only channel that you know anyway.

Why do you look at shows that show people with peculiar faces and strange vehicles? I don't like that crap, it doesn't make sense to me.

It makes sense to you because you are just like those stupid characters.

Why do you watch television, you can't follow what is going on? I don't feel like explaining everything to you that is happening on the television.

You are constantly asking me what is going on when we watch television.

Why do I have to tell you deed for deed, act for act when we are watching television?

Why can't you follow what is going on for yourself, it is so annoying?

You sit and watch Star Trek and that stupid History channel and I never come in and disturb you. Yet, you come in here with the story almost over and want me to tell you what is going on.

You would not understand it anyway so why disturb me with your dumb questions?

I think you need a hearing aid; you seem to hear only every third word that I say. You never hear the word no.

Are you too proud to wear a hearing aid, so that you will not keep asking me, "What did she say"?

Get a grip on life, old men need hearing aids and all other kinds of Aids.

Get a hearing aid. What do you want to do, turn the television up so it can be heard ten blocks away?

Now you want me to turn to a different channel so that you can go to sleep on it.

That is why you watch that stupid History channel. When we watch anything else you ask me a dozen questions about what is going on.

So you want to watch football, well, go in the other room or your study and watch it because you are not going to watch it in here.

Go to your room, turn the television to channel 57, the stupid History channel, sit in your chair and go to sleep and leave me alone.

Never mind, you are just being stupid, no one should watch television if they can't follow what is going on.

I told you that I don't want to watch the Star Trek movie, I don't care if it won twenty five academy awards and the best show of the year, I still don't want to watch it.

You watch that Star Trek movie for the tenth time if you want to, just leave me alone about it.

I think the television show is funny, you don't have to laugh or think its funny. You have no sense of humor anyway.

That brain of yours has too much unusable information in it to be normal.

Yes, you can watch television with me, just don't ask me any questions about what is going on.

You don't watch the other channels because you can't figure out what is going on. You always want me to explain what is happening.

Turn that television down and get a hearing aid, old man.

What's wrong with a hearing aid anyway.

There are televisions sets in every room in this house why do you come in here to watch television and disturb me.

I don't have to look at this and I don't want to look at it, so get out of here. You should not look at television, all you do is ask, "What's going on", you can't interpret anything that you see.

There are televisions sets all over this house so there is no need for you to come creeping in here.

If you don't want to watch what I am watching, go sit in you chair and got to sleep, you are at your best when you do that.

I am looking at what I want to look at and if you want to look at something else go in the study.

You have a two track mind, it is the History channel or the Star Trek channel, get a life.

Why are you so interested in the lady in the white blouse?

All this time you have been looking at the girl on television with the big tits and not the program. So stop asking me what's going on.

What difference does it make where I saw the movie, I saw it? It has been on television, which you never watch.

When you do watch television you are constantly asking me, "What is going on or what did he or she say?"

Are you going to watch television or act stupid.

No, I am not looking at that stupid Star Trek, why don't you just get up and get out of here and watch that dumb show in your study and leave me alone about it.

You come in here and complain about what I am watching. There are televisions in every room of this house. You are really a pain in the ass and all that you watch is Star Trek.

I don't know when Star Trek comes on and I don't care to know.

I am watching television just like you are, I just turned it on a few moments ago, so why are you asking me what is on.

You come in here and the television is on and you ask what are you looking at, and you want me to explain what is going on, get out of here and forget it.

You never watch television but you always want to know what is going on.

I don't want to watch the History channel because it does not interest me, if you want to watch it go in the other room.

Dinzel Washington is hot, what about you, you are just luke warm.

I forgot, you are too much of an idiot to hold a decent conversation. I may as well turn the television on since I can't have a meaningful conversation with you at the dinner table.

Are you listening to the news on the television? Every time some woman comes on you have to comment on how she looks.

Yes, you can come in here if you are not going to be asking me questions. No, you cannot come in here if you are going to be asking me questions about what is going on. Go out and buy yourself a hearing aid or get a large horn.

"Scotty beam me up, there is no intelligent life down here."

Time Together

> Ah, fill the Cup - what boots it to repeat
> How Time is slipping underneath our Feet:
> Unborn To-morrow and dead Yesterday,
> Why fret about them if To-day be sweet."
>
> *Rubaiyat of Omar Khayyam*

Men have no business staying home all the time.

I would rather have a companion who is intelligent and doesn't make inane remarks.

Your quality time includes me, so I don't want your quality time.

No! I don't want to spend any quality time with you, your quality time stinks.

I am perfectly relaxed while I am in this room alone, until you come in and disturb me.

You were gone three days and come back and ask if the cleaning ladies were here. Hell no, I don't make a mess of the house like you do when you are around. This morning I went to the bathroom and you had left the wet bath mat on the floor, your shaving cream on the counter and the tooth paste tube without its top.

You are still talking, and you have not heard a word that I said. In a few minutes you will be asking me what I said.

Where are you going? There goes that writing pad again.

I wish you could walk in my shoes and live with you one day, you would end up in an institution.

That man stood at the meeting and praised his wife, wasn't that nice. You would not understand why that is important.

I don't have anyone in this household that I can commiserate with. All you know how to do is take everything I say and write it down as farder for a damn book.

Every time you get into some activity you want to get me involved. I am not interested in your activities.

Those antique car club meetings are boring. I go just because of the dinner and I don't have to cook that day. If you want to get involved in something fine but just don't expect me to participate.

That book you wrote, "A Man and a Mule" is not "our" book. If it were my book or our book it would not have ended the way that it did.

"What's for dinner."

That is all that you can say, I can be talking to you and you cut me off and say, "What's for dinner?"

I am not going to Wilmington with you to any book signing. What do you expect me to do, stand around all day and watch you sign books.

I don't want to go shopping in Wilmington, you are just saying that to get me to go with you. You can forget it I am not going to any book signing with you, go by yourself.

You are hard to live with, anything that you think will annoy me you just do it.

I am sitting here on this couch minding my business, there are two couches in this room and you have to sit here and pester me.

I have a sense of humor, I just don't think what you are doing is funny, what you do is evil.

I don't care what you are going to say, I don't want to hear it.

All men do is sit around the house and ask what someone is doing.

Being your wife does not give you the right to disturb me.

You are getting really old and starting to repeat yourself too much. You have made that same statement five times during the past thirty minutes.

Can't a person have some privacy around here.

Its all about you, it's always all about you. Nothing in the whole world counts, but you.

No you don't! Just stay over there and mind your own business.

Stop creeping up behind me, ever time I look up there you are.

Find something to do except follow me around will you please.

No! stay in your shop and work I don't need your quality time.

Keep your quality time to yourself. I don't need your quality time. Your quality time just means that I get nailed and I don't want that.

How many times do I have to tell you that I don't want to spend any quality time with you. Your quality time usually ends up asking if you can nail me. Go in your study and leave me alone.

I don't want to spend any quality time with you, that is I don't want sex. That is your quality time.

You can't sit over here with me. Stay where you are.

So that you will not come creeping up on me, I am telling you that I am going to bed and I will be looking at television.

Do you ever see how calm and contented I am when I am sitting by myself. I think you do that just to pester me. Why come and sit and disturb my peace.

Get out, you don't have anything to do but bother me. I don't need this.

No, you can't sit over here with me. Stay where you are.

Here you come to sit by me. Sit over there in the other chair and leave me alone.

This is a hug, and this is a hug. Hugging is not about tit feeling and butt touching.

All that I have to say is, "I don't like something" and you will offer it to me.

Don't you wonder why I want to be alone? Why I go in a room by myself. It is to have some peace and to get away from you.

I really don't know how you can live with yourself, you should live alone or with another man.

That is the way it is, I get up and move and you have to follow.

Why are you following me? You and that damn cat always following me around. what do you want, forget it.

There is very little that I want to do, with you or for you.

You went out of town for a few days to play golf, thank you for my vacation.

It was just great being here alone, you should do that more often.

So you have been away for three days, look how neat everything is. Being away for three days does not mean that you have to nail me.

I even cleaned your desk. I had to wash it with soap and water.

Why do you have to announce that you are coming to spend quality time with me? What do I need with your quality time? I know what your quality time means and No! I don't want to have sex, today, tomorrow or forever.

I had a meaningful conversation with you at the dinner table, I don't need anymore.

Do you want something in here or are you just following me?

I am going to put a movie on so that you will stop following me and getting on my nerves.

Do I have to sit here and be disturbed by you, you don't know how to leave me alone? Get this, I want to be left alone and not disturbed.

To have to deal with you on a daily basis is sheer torture.

Haven't you noticed that I do things without you? Learn to do things by yourself and leave me alone.

I could really live without you, you see that I stay by myself all of the time.

What is it in your head that says you have to reach out and touch me?

If I pull this screen down one more time I will scream.

All the space and chairs in this room and you come and sit right on top of me.

Go sit in another chair, there is no room for you here.

Disturb you, that is the last thing that I would do.

Answer me! Is that the only reason that you pick on me, because you know that it annoys me?

No, I don't want to spend any quality time with you for the thousandth time.

You don't know what quality time is anyway.

Quality time is just being alone without you around bothering me.

I can do without this, you are annoying me and starting to get on my nerves. Just leave the room if you can't think of anything else to do.

No! I don't want to spend any quality time with you, when are you going to get that through your thick head.

Do I disturb you on a constant basis, No! I should be given the same treatment.

No, I don't want to play wife. Go find someone else to play wife with you and leave me alone.

You can come in the room and get in the bed but I am going to tell you this, stay on your side of the bed and don't put your pillow next to my head and don't start poking me.

The words that come out of your mouth are just childish, why don't you keep your mouth shut?

You have nothing to do so you decide that I will disturb my wife, get out and leave me alone.

Yes when you die, I just might cry, but I will not miss you picking on me.

I don't like it, I never did and I just want you to go out and leave me alone.

You think it's funny look at that smile on you face. I just want to sit here and be left totally alone.

Time alone and space are my only requests for this life and you will not give me either.

Helping Out

And that inverted Bowl we call the Sky,
Were under crawling coop't we live and die.
Lift not thy hands to It for help-for it
Rolls impotently on as thou or I.

Rubaiyat of Omar Khayyam

You are so accustomed to having people wait on you, you can do this yourself and by yourself.

You don't know how much I despise waiting upon someone.

Where in the hell do men get the idea that someone should wait upon them.

Can't you do something good just because it is the right thing to do. I guess that it is difficult for you to consider.

I don't ask you to do anything that I can do myself.

Do I need some help fixing dinner. Are you sick or something? No thank you. I don't need any help.

You go out and hire a firm to put vinyl siding on the damn house because you are too lazy to paint it. I think that is a waste of money and you could have painted the house.

This has gotten to be a habit, asking me for help.

Your help always involves something that I am not interesting in doing.

Helping out would be making the bed when you get out of it. You are the last one out of the bed and you should make it up.

I don't care when you are going to get back in it, it should be made up as soon as you get out of it.

I don't like the way that you make the bed anyway, you just pull the covers over the mess

That is not the way one should make a bed.

Did you make your bed that way when you were in the army, I don't think so?

I don't need your help, you are to old and arthritic to do anything but sleep.

What little help from you that I get around here I do not need.

To you the word help means, help me.

Mostly it means help me find something that I have misplaced in my dirty pottery shop or my office.

I am just a helpmate, not a wife or someone who is loved.

You bandy about the word "love" so much, I know that you don't have a clue as to its meaning.

I am going to move that trash container from near the dinner table.

Every time we sit here you reach back and try to put something in the trash container and you never look back to see where it is.

You just reach back and never look and it ends up on the floor.

I can't depend upon your word for anything. Am I supposed to read your mind.

You made a mess in the kitchen last night and left if for me to clean up.

You left the chair out and the dishes on the table, who do you think is going to clean up this mess.

I thought that would be done when I returned home, but it was not. It is only my job to fix meals while you sit around and do nothing.

Where do men get the attitude that they should be waited upon and then nail someone when they get the mood.

It takes two minutes to come over here and put the dishes in the dishwasher and you just leave them there. You don't have maids around here.

Don't sit there and wait to be waited upon, playing, King of the Hill."

You always take on a project for other people and then expect me to help. I am not your secretary or your maid.

I did not ask you for help, if there is something that needs doing I will do it myself.

You can't say please or thank you, it is do this, do that.

Everything that you are involved in, you expect help from me, you can forget it.

You are going to get the mail. Today is Sunday, hello!

The month is September and the year is 2006.

How old are you, half the time you can't even keep up with how old you are?

I was not put on this earth just to help an arthritic old man get through the day.

Can't you understand that I am not interested in your projects.

I don't like the people that attend your pottery shows, the people who attend are all phonies.

I need your help like I need a hole in the head.

Go find someone that needs your help and leave me alone.

Looking for Things

> For "Is" and "is" - Not" though with Rule and Line,
> And "Up - and - down" by Logic I define,
> Of all that one should care to fathom,
> I Was never deep in anything but -Wine.
>
> *Rubaiyat of Omar Khayyam*

*I*t has been said that most men spend one year of their lives looking for things.

You are always looking for something that you have misplaced, I could not live like that.

I think you have spent fifty years of your life looking for things.

Why don't you have a place to put things that you have and you would not have to spend so much time looking for them.

You know exactly where to find things in my office, because I keep all of my things in place. Yet you never put things back where they belong.

How do you think I knew where that was? I put it where I knew it belonged. I could find it even if I were blind.

When I need my things I can't find them because you never put them back where they belong.

Stand in the middle of the floor and ask, "Where is it?" You don't look for anything.

Yes, there is no point in looking for it, it will show up later somewhere or someplace.

Just because you can't find it, I was supposed to have moved it. I did not use it, you did, now look in that special place where you always put it, maybe the good fairy put it back.

The real reason why you can't find anything is because you have no special place to put anything. Yet you know where everything in my office is.

That is because I have a special place to put my things. My scissors, my pocketbook, my stamps, my paper, my tape and all the rest of my thing have their own special place. You could do the same thing, don't give me that "I am in tune with the universe because I seek disorganization." You are not in tune with anything that is why you are always looking for something.

No, I have not seen any of your pipes, the last time I smoked one of them I put them where they belong. Try putting things where they belong sometime and you would be able to locate them.

You have never looked for anything in your life. You just say "Where is my?"

You have a good memory, you just can't remember important things, like where something is.

Do you ever look for the matches that you have used or just go and get a new box?

What did you do with the tool that I gave you?

You look in the shop and I will look in the garage, there is no need for you to follow me and look in the same place that I am looking.

Do you want me to look for this or you just want to act like a simpleton?

Are you still opening that drawer and looking for your socks and underwear? Your socks and underwear have not been in that drawer for five years.

You said you looked in the garage. It was right on the shelf.

Five percent of your life is spent looking in the rear view mirror, can you change the past, if not forget it?

There is nothing that you can do about the past when is your little brain going to realize that.

The other ninety five percent of your life is spent looking for something that you have misplaced and asking where some of your possession are located.

You spend half of your life looking for things and the other half asking me where something is.

I can't have a day without you losing something and asking, "Where is my?"

You could have found this yourself, you are sitting there and waiting for me to wait on you.

It is always me that you come to find something that you have misplaced and you misplace everything that you own.

I don't know how you can love yourself, much less live with yourself.

I don't understand you, why can't you leave things alone if you can't leave them where you find them.

I asked you a question, do you think you can answer it or are you just going to sit there like a bump on a log.

It must make you feel good to always be asking or looking for something, and never having any idea of where your possessions are located.

What is this, I have to tell you what is what. Where is where? Are you so dopey that you can't keep up with anything.

You would really be bored to death if you did not have me to pick on and find the things that you misplace.

You don't keep up with anything. It is a good thing that your head is attached to your body otherwise you would lose it.

Your entire life is one big Easter egg hunt. You are forever looking for something and you can't keep up with anything.

You stand in the middle of the room and expect me to find something for you.

I don't understand how anyone as inept as you can live with themselves. You never know where anything is or what is up or down.

I don't have a clue as to where whatever you are looking for is located. Maybe if you would just learn to have a special place for your things you would not spend your whole life looking for them.

Did you find it there? just put it back where it belongs and the next time you will not have to look for it or ask me where it is.

I wonder where you found that jelly, it was on the middle shelf and not on the top shelf. The jelly stays on the middle shelf, please try to remember that.

When you go to look for it you will have to ask me where it is.

Do you know what it's like to have to live with someone who is totally disorganized, to live with someone who can't keep up with anything?

You don't know which end is up.

You walk around in a daze not knowing where anything is.

You waste you life because ninety percent of it is spent looking for things.

You except to be waited on, go get it yourself if you want it. I don't feel like looking for it for you.

Don't expect me to find it for you. What do I ask you to find for me, nothing?

Your tobacco pouch is on the hassock in the study. Of course you don't look for anything. You just stand in the middle of the room and say "Where is my?"

Why don't you try looking for something yourself?

It would be better still if you put things where they belong and you would no have to look for them.

So you are trying to reduce the time spent out of your life looking for things by asking me to find them. I guess that makes sense to you but it makes no sense to anyone else.

I have a special place for my things and you should have a special place for your things. No!, You just leave things all over the place.

I know where your son gets his bad habits. He gets them from you.

If I could not keep up with my things it would drive me crazy and the two of you go through life happy as larks and as loony as you can be.

I can't believe that the two of you can live like that and spend most of you lives looking for thing.

Neither of you know how to close drawers, turn off lights or put things where they belong and the two of you are always looking for something.

Your son is a product of his father, he can never find anything. It is because neither of you are organized and put things where they belong when you finish using them.

You son is just like you, you never set the correct example. You should have taught him how to organize. Now he never puts things back where they belong when he has finished with them.

Where is my, where is my, that is all that I hear from you?

I did not touch anything of yours so don't ask me, "Where is my?"

Who moved those things out of here? There are only two of us living here and I like things placed where they belong. If you felt that way you would not have to always be looking for things and saying, "Where is my?" That is because you don't have any place for your things, and that is why you can never find anything.

You should always have a place for all of your tools and you would then know where they are, but knowing you, you would never place them where they belong anyway.

That thing has been sitting on the table for three or four days and you ask, "where is my?" Do you ever look before you ask or do you just ask out of habit?

Did you look in the refrigerator for the cheese or did you just open the refrigerator door and say, "Where are you cheese?"

Has it ever occurred to you that you could find something yourself, rather than sit on your butt and ask someone else to find it?

You spend half your life looking for things.

Why don't you put your things in a special place where you would know where they are? Then you might remember where they are and not always be looking for them.

You want to make yourself a better person, then get organized and put your things where they belong.

Keep up with your things, you addle brain.

Now you can't find your check book, why don't you keep it where it belongs.

I am tired of this, go look for your check book yourself and leave me alone.

All you ever say is, "Where is my and can you fix me?"

Sure my brain works better than yours, you never know where anything is.

You are the most pathetic person I have ever seen, you can't do anything or find anything.

You are really getting bad, you can't find anything. Why don't you keep up with your things? You are so addlebrained.

Its odd that you knew exactly where to find that but you didn't put it back in my office where you found it.

You leave something in every place that you go.

Here are your shoes, you will be looking for them later.

Why should I dial that number? You have hands and if you can find your glasses, do it yourself. No, I will not look for your glasses.

I don't know where your glasses are. The last time I wore them I put them where they belong.

It was really nice being here by myself without you messing up the place and asking me where everything that you own is located.

Nothing is sacred in this house you just walked out with my fish food.

I brought the fish food for my fish not for yours, buy your own fish food.

If you had a special place for your glasses you would not lose them.

You lost them and now you want to Blame me, forget.

I was looking for the chocolate syrup and found it in the freezer.

You put it there after you ate your cream, don't you ever know where things belong?

No, I don't feel sorry for you. You are the one who can't keep up with anything,

I think someday you will lose your name.

You had the nerve to say last night that there was no ice in the ice tray. What in the hell do you expect if you use all the ice in the ice tray and never refill them.

Do you realize that most of your life is spent looking for things that you have misplaced. Doesn't that bother you just a little bit.

I don't know where yours are but I know where mine is because I put my things where they belong after I use them.

You spend all of your time looking for things that you have misplaced. Get a grip on the real world and try to do the impossible, get organized.

You haven't put that back yet, that is the way things get lost, when you use something you should put it back, otherwise it gets lost.

Where is my, where is my, where is my? That is what your are always saying. If you put your things where they belong you would not be always saying, "Where is my?"

Your class ring is in the flower room by the second flowerpot. If you learned to put things in a special place you would not always be looking for them.

You are a totally disorganized person.

Growing up back in that woods without playmates did a job on you.

Should I put this someplace where you can find it later or leave it here so you can lose it?

Why is this in the middle of the floor, so that some one can break a leg on it or so that you can find it?

You really have a bad case of CRS {can't remember shit}.

I love it, you actually found something yourself?

I am going to start calling you, "Where is my?" or "What's wrong?"

I paid a lot of money for that coat, you are too cheap to buy one yourself and now you have lost it.

I know with your mixed up brain that you have no idea where it is.

I should put your name in your coat because you always lose things.

I still think we should put your name on your clothes like I used to do my kindergartners so that you could keep up with them.

No, I don't expect you to look for the damn coat, you will just go to Wal-Mart and buy another cheap one.

I said when you left here, "The only place where your coat could be would be outside in that dirty kiln shop."

That is where I found it.

Wife, wife, wife, wife… and it always ends with where is my, where is my, where is my?

How do I always find my things, its because I put them where they belong.

I am an orderly person, I keep up with my things and you should try to do the same. If you keep up with your things you would not have to use mine.

There are things that I am not supposed to remember, look up the damn phone number yourself. What would you do if I were not around?

Yes, I have my claw hammer in my office. I found it in that dirty shop of yours filled with clay after you removed it from my office without asking. You will notice the note on the
handle. The note says, "wife's hammer."

I could never be like you, totally disorganized and always looking for things. I could never spend my whole life looking for my possessions.

That is no way to live.

I have told you many times that you should have a special place to place your keys and your bag and all I get is "Where is my?"

A wife is not someone who is around just to locate your lost items. The older you get the less you remember. What would you do if I were not around to find your possessions?

You would spend all of you time looking for them.

Please stay out of my office there is nothing in there that belongs to you.

I purchased all of the supplies and stamps in my office for my use.

Try to remember that my office is not Staples or Office Depot. Those are the places where you will find the supplies that you need.

Love

Me with penis envy, surely you jest. I have two pieces of meat hanging from my chest, I sure don't want a thrid one.

Ah, Love! could thou and I with Faith conspire
To grasp this sorry Scheme of Things entire,
Would not we shatter it to bits-and then
Re-mould it nearer to the Heart's Desire?

Rubaiyat of Omar Khayyam

Life would have been far less complicated if I had ignored the boy on the streetcar stop.
I didn't and here we are two old people still trying. Happy Valentines Day. I love you in spite of the way you are.

Sure you love me, I am your maid, your servant, your "find my," and then I get nailed.

I don't think you could change the way that you are even if you wanted too.

You have to show me that you love me and not just saying it, that doesn't cut it.

I used to love the way you touched me, now you are old and droopy and I wish you would not.

Yes, you love me because if it were not for me you would be lost and you would never find anything.

You don't understand the word "love" and you have no idea of what it means.

Just because you think that I have pretty legs, pretty arms, a pretty face, pretty hair and big tits doesn't mean that you deserve a kiss or that I get nailed.

You are crazy. I don't want the first bit of what you call loving, anyway I call it juking around and I am not interested in juking around.

Me, with penis envy, surely you jest, I have two pieces of meat hanging from my chest I sure don't want a third one.

You don't love anyone but your damn self, so stop saying, " I love you." It doesn't mean a thing.

Picking and pulling on me is not "love". You are in love with yourself and no one else.

You take after your mother, she had a fetish for love, get out of here and leave me alone.

No! I don't want a hug from you, you are not a nice person.

I made a big mistake when I married you.

I don't care what you think, you are not going to get anything from me. I don't feel like getting nailed tonight or the next night.

You don't have a clue as to what making love is. Making love is not just sex.

Loving to you means sex and not two minutes of it, it is more like two hours.

All I want is to be reassured that you are a human being but you never act like one.

So you do that because you love me, you know I don't like you touching my tits, so what would be a reasonable thing to do if you loved me.

You don't know what love is and that is why you don't get lucky.

I don't go for that "I love you" stuff. Love doesn't mean waiting upon you.

"If you don't do this it means you don't love me!" You are damn right.

You are not going to blackmail me with that crap.

Marriage!, I will never make that mistake again if I live a thousand years.

Yes! You have a favorite and it is you. Sure you are concerned about my cold, I can tell by looking at your face, you have a sneer all over it.

No! I don't want you to touch me, you do that just for yourself, you don't know what affection is.

There is love in your heart? The fact is, I don't think you have a heart.

There is nothing gentle about you, when they say gentleman, its not about you.

The Lord did not put you on earth to be a pain, maybe he did.

You are not a creature of habit, you are a bad habit.

Just because I have on a pretty sweater, that doesn't mean that I deserve a hug from you.

Someone who has been in the house all day and walks by and says, "Hi love", what am I supposed to say.

You have been gone one half day and you ask if I missed you, hell no!

You are not a creature of habit, You just do the same thing over and over because you don't realize that you have done it before, Mr. CRS.

I love the way you sit at my desk and go through my things, go search through your own desk.

At least some one remembered my special day, my birthday, but you didn't, you had to wait until you heard me talking about it on the phone.

The only time I have no pain is when I go to sleep and then you come in with all that noise, waking me up, talking to me and turning on the bright lights. You call that loving me.

That's your problem, you think that giving things is affection, never mind just go into your pottery shop and work.

No! I don't love you, that has long since passed.

I really don't think that even your mother loved you.

You inherited your mother's way of loving yourself.

You are best at indulging yourself. You have no respect for me. People who love themselves can't love others and you are completely involved with yourself.

Come back when you learn what love really is and maybe something will happen. I might even let you nail me.

The Pottery Shop

Listen again. One Evening at the Close
Of Ramazan, ere the better Moon arose,
In that old Potter's Shop I stood alone
With the clay population round in Rows.

Rubaiyat of Omar Khayyam

What! You work in your pottery shop to support your wife?

Surely you jest.

I didn't put clay in here, you are the one who works in clay.

No! "We", don't have to go to the art reception.

You come up with that "we" shit, we have to do this, we have to do that, we don't have to do anything.

No, I'm not going. I am no going because I don't want to go.

You are so busy thinking about what people think, who cares. I don't need other people's approval, I have my own approval.

You are extremely wishy-washy, one minute you say you have all the money you need and the next you are rushing to make pottery to sell.

I still think that you make fifty cents an hour considering the time you spend in that dirty shop.

Considering the time that you spend in that pottery shop, I estimate that you make less than fifty cents an hour.

Big "W" Hobbies might be an important company, but the CEO doesn't tell anyone when someone is coming over, like I don't live here.

You are not a CEO. CEO's have people working for them and you have no money and no employees.

Does that make you feel important being CEO of a stupid pottery company.

Yes, you are the CEO, but all your employees have quit, and the poor CEO has to do all the work including scrubbing the floor.

CEO's have people doing that kind of work.

You are a CEO, I don't think so, That is like saying that you are head of a company and you still scrub the floors.

You might be the CEO but your company has one person and no employees. You are the one who does all the work, if that is your definition of a CEO go for it.

Me get a job at McDonalds because you claim you are the CEO of some nonexistent company. You can forget that one.

I don't have a job? What are you talking about? I have a job. My job is keeping my self sane and staying out of your way as much as possible.

So you are the CEO of that Mickey Mouse Company, that is some kind of cruel joke. You have no employees, no hired help, you do all the work, scrub the floors, and make a mess with your pottery and you call yourself a CEO.

Why do you need a title to feel important.

Why do you always have to be touching and feeling? When I am sitting here minding my business, enjoying the quietness and you enter and start pestering me. Go back to your company Mr. CEO with no workers.

You don't have a job, you have a hobby that makes money and no, I do not have a job. I don't need a job with you around you are my job.

You have to give everyone that spiel about your pottery.

"I don't do it for the money, I do it to satisfy my need to be creative." That is pure bull.

That is a bad joke, your first thought when you get up in the evening from bed is how much money do I have? How many pots did I sell yesterday?

You close the bedroom door but you always leave your shop door opened and all the warm air goes in there.

That pottery shop door is sitting open every morning when I get up. Do you know how to close it?

You have clay or something all over the floor. When I get up in the morning it is all over the place and you say I don't have a job. Why don't you take my place for a short while? You would see which of us has a real job and it would not be you.

Disturbing me is your one job in life.

You don't even make the minimum wage.

Count all the time that you spend in that shop and the money that you pay for supplies and electricity and figure how much per hour you make, it is about thirty cents or less.

You work in your pottery shop to hide from me, thank you.

Why is your shop door opened? I have closed it a dozen times during the past week.

I don't want to look in that dirty shop and I don't want anyone else to have to look at it.

You are working in the pottery shop with your good clothes on. You have no respect for anything.

You have old clothes that you can wear when working in your shop.

Every room in this house contains your mess except your shop where it belongs.

Why don't you put something old on when you are working in the shop? Don't say that clay is not dirty.

Stupid man, used his good pants in that dirty shop, a waste of money to buy you anything nice.

Get dirty and say, "It will come out", it will not get clean.

Do you know how embarrassing it is for me to see you go out with clay and crap all over you? People see the females as the ones who do the laundry.

Yes, I'll bet you have a job, anyway you need another one, and you have too much time on your hands.

So you are a potter and you have a job, I don't think so, your only job is to meddle with what I am doing.

Jeeze, you work? You are either on that computer or in you shop, you call that work.

I am retired and so are you, old man.

If I did get a job the first thing that I would do is leave this place. I am tired of putting up with your shit and you picking on me.

What do I want with that piece of pottery? It is temporary anyway, you will sell it eventually. There are only a few pieces that I have managed to keep.

I don't want any of your pots, they are all over the house in places where they don't belong. Anyway, you will sell them as soon as you run out of pots to sell.

Do you have another wife because you don't support me?

You are best at indulging your self?

Sure you are in tune with the universe. That is why you get ripped off in your pottery business dealings. It is because you are so disorganized.

You have on your good clothes, would you please change them before you go into that pottery shop? You will get clay all over the clothes that you have on and you are not the one who washes them

Please close the door to your shop. Who wants to look at that dirty shop?

Do you think I care if you go out to that pottery shop all day? I don't, at least you are out of my way and not picking on me.

Just go into your potter shop and work for your fifty cents and hour. Considering the time you spend in there that is about all you make.

Go to your pottery shop or find something to do. I need my space.

No! I don't want to go the Art Gallery, how many times do I have to say that? I don't like those people there they are not my kind of people.

When did I discuss going to the Art Gallery, never, you must have dreamed it?

Why would you clean your potters shop, you are accustomed to the mess in there?

Get out of my face and go find something to do that will keep you busy. I don't need you following me around the house like some little child.

Take a good look at your class ring, what do you see on it - clay.

Get out of here and leave me alone, go to you pottery shop and play with your clay.

You might be a good potter but you are a sorry person.

Doesn't it bother you to be here all day meddling with what I am doing? I think you need to make some more pots.

What kind of pleasure would I get out of that, watching you make pots? Just get out of here and leave me alone.

I watched you make pots when I was young and I don't see the need to come into your shop and watch you make pots.

Why should I come in there and watch you play in the mud, that pottery shop is a disaster anyway?

Why do you need your wife in your shop, you have two wives both of them are working with clay right now?

In order of importance you think you are number one, two, three, four and your pottery items are number five.

I am calling to let you know that we arrived safely. I am not going to stop at any construction site and get any red clay for you. If your son, can find some around here that is well and good, but I refuse to stop at any construction site and get red clay.

You would make a mess of anything, not just your pottery shop.

Around The House

> And, as the Cock crew, those who stood before
> The Tavern shouted- "Open then the Door.
> You know how little while we have to stay,
> And, once departed, may return no more."
>
> *Rubaiyat of Omar Khayyam*

I changed the house around six months ago and you are still bumping into things.

I changed this room around six months ago and you are still complaining about it, you had better get used to it because it is going to stay that way for a while and then I will change it again.

I don't like a boring house so I change the furniture around. It has nothing to do with you. You would not be able to find your way around anyway.

You keep looking in that drawer for your socks and they

have not been in that drawer for five years. I would put a note of the drawer that contains your socks, but I don't think that would help. Get a grip on life.

Why don't you pay attention to things around you?

Just do the dishes, OK, nothing else.

I have never before in my life seen anyone who each time he sits down he knocks the telephone off the hook.

Don't try to fix the dishwasher. I want someone to work on it who knows what he or she are doing. I don't want you fiddling around with it.

When are you going to paint the inside of the house?

We have been here for twenty years and it has never been painted. No! don't hire someone to do it. You and your son can paint the damn house.

I asked you just once to paint the outside of the house and you had someone put vinyl siding on it because you didn't want to paint it. That cost twelve thousand dollars, just because you are too lazy to paint the damn house. Well thank you, it looks better than it would have if you had tried to paint it.

What are you going to do now, have someone put vinyl siding on the inside of the house?

Just buy the paint and start painting and see if it kills you to do it.

You never open things the right way, you were supposed to open the package so that it could be closed and sealed again. What you did was just rip off the top of the package.

I will put your check out in the hallway for the house cleaner. I hope she comes soon as I will be away for a few days. The house cleaner might not be able to get in the door to do the cleaning with your mess all over the place.

I know where things are in the house because my mind is not cluttered with useless facts and I think with my brain. You should try it sometime.

Sure you can quote poetry for five hours but you can't find a single one of your tools. It is a good thing that your head is attached otherwise I would have to find it for you.

Do you realize that you are klutzy?

You come in here and disturb me and sit too close to me, you short bus person.

The house cleaner said that you made the bed.

She stated, "Your husband made the bed, bless his soul."

How does she know that you made the bed? She knows by the way the bed looks, it was a mess.

Just do the dishes, and keep your mouth shut. I don't want to hear your dumb comments about women's work. There is no such thing.

I am not too lazy to clean up after myself.

People in this house don't understand that they should clean up after themselves, after they mess up the place.

We are "people" and the two of us live in this pig sty because you don't know how to keep things neat and tidy.

If you cleaned up right after you made a mess I would not have to look at it.

You turn it on, you turn it off.

You open, it you close it.

Here we go again. You take all the ice from the tray, doesn't it occur to you to fill it with water in order to make more ice.

Must you turn the ice tray upside down to remove the ice. Don't you realize that the ice is going to fall on the floor and then I will have to clean up the mess.

Maybe, just maybe, you will clean up the mess this time.

I don't want to hear, "I am sorry." Just clean up behind yourself and don't leave your mess all over the house.

The Cars And Driving

> Indeed the Idols I have loved so long
> Have done my credit in this World much wrong:
> Have drown'd my Glory in a shallow Cup,
> And sold my reputation for a song.
>
> *Rubiayat of Omar Khayyam.*

I don't like old cars and I am not interested in hearing people talk about them, as if they are the greatest things in the world.

No, you don't have to eat the same thing tomorrow and the only reason is because we are going to a party with your antique car club.

We are going to the store, how many other places do you have to go?

Whenever I'm driving you want me to chauffeur you all over the place.

Don't write on anything that I have in my car.

No! I don't want to ride in that model A Ford, that car is older than I am. Why would I want to ride in something that old.

I looked all over for your hammer and finally I went to the tool kit in my car and got mine. I always know where my tools are.

Why did you park the van on this side of the driveway? I don't want you to open the van door on the side where my car is. I don't want you to hit my car with the door. I try to keep my car free of dents. I don't want it to end up like yours.

You did not teach me to drive a car, you tried to teach me to drive a car.

You did not teach me to drive a car, you keep saying that, you tried to teach me to drive a car. You don't know how to drive properly, so how could you teach someone else to drive.

Your shit is all over my car, I don't understand why people ruin other people's property. I am "people" that's who.

I will go with you but I will only go in my car, your car is dirty and there is no place to sit.

I will drive because you never have your mind on what you are doing when you drive and you never pay attention to your driving. I want to live a little longer and not die when you have an accident.

I don't put trash in there, I told you that once. That is why your car is so dirty. You put trash anywhere.

You are in my car and I am driving. First it is too cold and then it is too hot, make up your mind.

You might be intelligent, but you don't know a damn thing about cars.

Don't ask anyone for directions, just keep driving and we will end up in Europe or some other place.

What is wrong with asking for direction if you are lost?

Is not asking for directions some male macho thing?

No, you just keep on going thinking the right way will show up.

We are going to the store, how many other places do you have to go? You need a chauffeur or a designated driver, I am neither.

It is annoying that you think you know so much, on the trip to Washington, the Expedition red light came on. There was something wrong with the car but Mr. know-it-all said, "There is nothing wrong with the car, that light comes on when you reach a certain number of miles." Then we had car trouble.

Get in your car and go to those places yourself. You know how to drive, I think.

How do I know where it is? It was in the car, you leave everything in the car, and it is always a mess.

Every time I go out in the car you have to ask where I'm going and then list a dozen places that you want me to go.

Why can't you go to those places when you are out and driving?

Now you tell me to turn, you tell me at the last minute to make a right turn. What do you expect me to do turn on a dime?

You answer yes, and you don't know if the car has oil or gas.

Your saying yes is just telling me to shut up.

You made a mess of the car, look at your hands they have clay all over them.

It is time for you to be leaving. or are you going to wait until the last minute and then rush out and have an accident?

Did you go online and get directions to where you are going? There is a right way and a wrong way to do things.

Where are you going? You have to find your car keys first.

No! we will not go for the car until I get a call from the auto shop. It is the same when we went to your brother-in-laws home.

You said you had called and he was at home but when we got there, no one was at home.

I like to understand what is happening or going to happen. You don't have a clue to where you are going.

I told you once before, we are not going to the repair shop. We will not go for the car until I get a call from the auto shop. Is there something wrong with your hearing or can't you understand a simple statement?

I don't like surprises and I like directions as to where we are going.

It is always the same with you, don't know where you are going, don't ask directions, just keep driving and the car will find its way.

Watch where you are driving, you should be in the other lane.

Why don't you pay attention to what you are doing?

You wonder why I always do the driving. It is because you never have your mind on what you are doing or where you are going.

I don't want to be involved in an accident with your dumb driving habits.

That Austin Healey 3000 of yours is just like you, a pain in the ass. Something is always wrong with it. Just as there is something wrong with you.

You can hardly get in and out of that Austin Healey, old man, why don't you just sell it.

Both you and that Austin Healey 3000 are old, bent over and ready for the graveyard. It is not a car for two old people like you and me.

You have an attachment to that Austin Healey, you have been selling it for the last twenty years.

You have had that Austin Healey for forty years, don't you think that is long enough.

You will never sell it. When you die, I will sell it in a hot minute.

No, I don't want to go with you, I don't want to ride in that Austin Healey, that car is a pain to drive and to ride in for old people like us.

You brought that Model A Ford and you do not know how to fix it. You grew up with a bicycle for household transportation. You know next to nothing about repairing cars.

Don't go through the papers in this car, you are screwing up my system?

We will go in the green van, your car is too dirty with all that crap on the floor.

Don't wait until the last minute and then drive like a crazy man.

Did you tell me that you wanted to go there before we left the house? I would suggest that the next time you take your own car when we go out.

My father always took care of his cars he didn't wait until they stopped running like you do.

You should get the mirror on your van fixed before you have an accident. Why can't you take care of necessary things and repairs to your vehicles?

Go away! Can't you see that I am trying to drive the damn car.

Listen, if your brother-in-law doesn't want you to put ashes in the ashtray of his car, just remember that it is his car and not yours.

Like most poor people, his car is his most prized possession.

CRS: Can't remember shit, again, I told you a week ago that I was going to visit my sisters on Thursday.

Did you think to bring the jump cables or to put the cars out of the driveway, I don't think so?

I don't think that you think about anything that is important. You have too much sex on your mind to think about anything that is important like your driving habits.

Have you ever heard of the short bus, well this house is the funny farm?

You talk about driving, you are without a doubt the world's worst driver.

God looks out for babies and fools, and you are no baby. That is the only reason you have not had an accident, it is only that God looks out for babies and fools.

No! I don't want any loving, as if you know what loving really is, anyway, what could you do in the car old man?

Why don't you watch where you are driving and get your mind out of the gutter? No, we will not stop at a motel and anyway what would we do there.

You never pay attention to your driving or anything else for that matter.

Where are you going for car keys?

I know where you are going.

You are going to my closet to get the spare set.

Why don't you keep up with your car keys? You will just lose that set of car keys and then what will you do.

What key did you use when you drove your car today? Did you look for your keys or did you go in my closet and get the safe set of keys?

You went into the closet again and got the spare key because you could not find yours and you are too lazy to look for them. Why can't you keep up with anything?

The inside of the Lincoln Town car is a mess.

When I drove the Lincoln it was always clean.

You should look at the inside of that car, there is junk every where.

You are a shit head and you don't take care of your car or anything else.

You didn't wash your car even when you were young, your mother always said, you were the only one who came down with a dirty car.

Are you going to have space to sit in that car with all the junk on the seat?

Sorry, means nothing to you, it means "shut up", it's what little children say when they want to be left alone.

Why did you drive my car? I don't want my car to be a mess like yours.

All you know how to do is drive the car, cleaning it is not on your agenda.

One of these day you are going to hit the arm on the security gate.

You make a mess of what you love, how can you make such a mess of that car. That car is a filthy mess.

You have a hard time keeping up with the time, you are always in a rush. You are an accident looking for a place to happen.

We have an hour and a half so you don't have to rush to get back for the New Years Eve Party.

You want to drive my car because you are too cheap to pay $2.50 for a gallon of gas.

So you remember when gas was 16.9 cents a gallon, when was that, in the year one? Times have changed but you have not. Gas prices have not been that low in recorded history.

Do I look as stupid as a Watford? Do you see stupid written on my forehead. The weather forecast is for a hurricane with flooding and you think that I am going to drive someplace.

You live in a different world. There is a hurricane today and the pro shop is closed. Who do you think is going to go there anyway?

You missed the turn and drove miles out of the way. Why can't you keep your mind on your driving.

You thought, you thought nothing, you were not paying attention to your driving as usual.

You can't remember where you have been even if you had gone there yesterday.

Please don't put ashes in the ash tray in my car. That might be what ash trays are for, but not in my car.

The minute I get in the car you have a dozen places for me to go. Why can't you drive to the store and pick up all those items that you want and then go to the post office and the hardware store?

Do I have on a chauffeur's uniform? I am not going to drive you all over creation. You have a car, why don't you use it? You can't afford the gas? What do you think my car uses, water?

Organization

> Ah, my Beloved, fill the Cup that clears.
> To-day of past Regrets and Future Fears.
> To - morrow! - Why, To - morrow I my may be;
> Myself with Yesterday's Sev'n thousand years.
>
> *Rubiayat of Omar Khayyam*

You are not a good business man. All the people that you deal with take advantage of you because you are so disorganized.

Never knowing where anything is and always looking for something. Think of how much of your life is spend just looking for things that you have misplaced. You have the worst case of CRS {can't remember shit} in the whole world.

Why can't you be just a little bit organized?

I don't give a damn about the universe seeking disorder, I am talking about you.

I really don't think your elevator goes up to the top floor. If it did you would be more organized.

"Give me a break." This is a different world altogether not the unorganized world that you live and write in.

Look at the bills that you have paid twice. Why can't you organize your accounts and stop making errors.

We should have four tables in the dinning room and I will bet that they would all be full of your junk.

You still claim that you are in tune with the universe because you are disorganized.

Who wants to be in tune with a disorganized universe except you?

Being disorganized does not mean you are scientific or in tune with the universe. You use that entropy shit to cover your bad habits. You are disorganized because you are a slob.

I don't want to be in tune with the universe if it means that I bungle my way through life, never knowing where anything is or what is going on around me.

I could not go through life always looking for something or asking someone where something is.

Have you noticed that I never ask you where any of my things are? Do you know why I don't ask? I keep up with my possessions and I don't suffer from CRS {Can't remember shit}.

If you want your life to be disorganized that is fine with me but don't go in my office looking for anything. I have my office organized like a normal person.

You want to live with my order and your disorder, it will not work. Stay out of my office there is nothing in there that you purchased or that belongs to you. I keep my office ordered and you should do the same.

You have your nerve, talking about entropy, you are not the universe, Mr. can't find shit.

Wouldn't your life be simpler, if you were organized? Think of how much time in the last week that you have spent looking for things. That is no way for a person to go through life, always looking for something or asking where something is.

You really don't care about organization as long as you have a flunky who will look for things for you, you will always be a disorganized person saying, "Where is my?"

You are too old and set in your ways to make any significant changes in your life or the way that you are. You will continue to bungle your way through life.

You didn't put those things back where you found them; do you want me to do it?

It just takes a little time to organize things.

I had a pad on the table to write notes on and it is gone and I know that you are the one who moved it. The person who moved it was Mr. Unorganized, who can't find his way out of a paper bag.

You need a damn secretary to help you get organized.

Please don't mess up my desk; everything here has to be neat for me. I don't know how you work at your desk. All that mess on your desk would drive me crazy.

There is something wrong up there, your clock stopped before the hour.

I am not your damn secretary and I don't get paid to be one. Do it yourself. You have two hands.

No, you live here so I don't live alone. I have a thorn in my house that keeps trying to stick me.

You would lose your head if it were not attached, get organized if that is possible for you.

See if you can keep it in that small-unorganized brain of yours.

Don't be going through my stuff, that does not belong to you, my office is organized and everything has a place.

You should get your office organized and then you would not have to be looking through my stuff.

Do I look like your secretary? You come up with write that letter, who do you think you are talking to; you don't have a secretary, remember that.

You take the writing pads and never put them back, you must have a stack of them in your unorganized office.

As soon as I close my eyes you shove something in my face to proofread, then turn on the bright lights.

Would you please get a damn secretary?

You want me to answer so that you can write it down. Well write that you are totally self-serving, unorganized and can't keep up with a damn thing.

If you join that organization you are going to try to pull me in, read this, read that. I really don't care what happens to that organization. I want no part of it.

We now have six more months of work with that organization and then we are out of it.

I am tired of you and the organizations.

Don't write on those pads, I don't have anything to write

telephone numbers on. Find you own pads in that unorganized office of yours.

Judy the television lawyer wrote in her book that if, your son-in-law, did not call her his balls would fall off. I wonder if he wrote that in his book. Mr. unorganized.

If you can't fix it, leave it alone.

Your book and your writings are as disorganized as you are and you are totally disorganized.

People will look at this and say, "This woman has to deal with this crazy unorganized man and you are crazy as a loon."

Did you write down that you are grumpy and that you can't do anything, that you are totally disorganized, with a smile on your face?

What happened to the paper pad that I had by the telephone? I try to organize things but you do not help.

You are always writing shit down. When are you going to quit? If you were not so busy writing dumb remarks, you might be able to find some of your possessions.

If you were more organized you could keep up with your tools and you would not have to use mine.

So you would do the necessary work around the house if you had the tools like the guy on television, I'll bet you would.

If you had the tools like the guy on television, you would not know where to find them.

You keep your tools all over the place and you can never find anything that you need, not even a hammer.

Listening

> Myself when young did eagerly frequent,
> Doctor and Saint, and heard great argument;
> About it and about: but evermore
> Came out by the same door as in I went.
>
> *Ruhaiyat of Omar Khayyam*

Were you listening to me, no, you were half listening? I will have to repeat what I said.

That word "no" means nothing to you It seems to always get it confused with the word, "maybe". I am saying No! No! No! and I mean, hell No!

Your head is so filled with yourself that you don't listen to me. I told you that I was going to get flu shots today and that is what I'm going to do.

Do you ever listen to me? I don't think so.

Just shut up, listen to yourself, you don't know how to fuss and that is not the way that I do it. I tried to teach you but you can't learn. You talk too fast and move your hands. I don't do that. I just calmly say what I am going to say. Forget it, you will never learn to fuss, you are impossible.

Listen carefully to what I am going to say. You take the door knob and pull it towards you and that will close the door. Do you understand that?

You never listen, everything that I say goes right through your ears.

I don't feel like listening to that, don't blame anyone but yourself.

Sometimes you don't listen to me. I can say anything because you are the way that your are, you never listen or pay attention to what I am saying.

Listen carefully to what I am going to say. I am not interested in getting nailed, the answer is no and it doesn't mean maybe.

Who in the hell wants to listen to Shakespeare's Hamlet. You are the only idiot that I know of that wants to listen to that shit.

When I talk and you say "Yep", I know that you are not listening to a word that I say.

You never listen to what I am saying, you go off on another subject as easy as peeing.

Let me talk to you, process! process! I am talking to you. I am talking to you so listen.

Do you ever listen to what you are saying, you repeat yourself a lot. It's as if people can remember the first time {People happens to be me}.

Just a few minutes ago I said, "no one listen to me." Now you repeat it thank you.

I said no, hell no, go to you dirty pottery shop and use up your excess energy.

I am not listening to you. Don't you know that? Do you think that you are Dan Rather or some other commentator?

I sometime feel like having you repeat what I said like I used to do to my kindergarten students. I don't think you are ever listening to what I am saying.

I have to listen to a broken record that got stuck in one spot

It is always find this, find that, where is my, don't you ever look for something yourself?

You say "Yes" to anything that I ask you. You are not even listening to me.

You don't hear what I am saying; you are so busy making jokes. When you have something important to say, which is seldom, I listen to you.

"She could get a franchise to manufacture General Motors Cars and she is with him." How many times do I have to hear that? You have been saying that for fifty years, the same statement over and over. It seems that an intelligent person would think of something else to say.

I don't talk to hear myself talk, I may as well, you never listen to what I say. I still think all old men should be required to wear hearing aids.

You still have a single joke in your repertoire and I don't want to hear it for the one thousandth one time.

You did not hear me; you are too busy with that dumb joke.

If you ever have something important to say, I try to listen and respond.

You don't ever listen to me, I was sitting there and I told you what to do and it passed right through your two ears.

Are you listening to me or writing down some more of that shit for that dumb book?

Just listen to the television and see if you can figure out what is going on and not ask me about it.

I never have to explain the show when you are watching and listening to Star Trek or that dumb History channel.

I think you hear and know what is going on and you just want to disturb me.

How can I listen to the program and explain it to you at the same time?

Listen to what I'm saying, I don't want to watch a movie with you. How many times do I have to say that?

I don't waver and don't use all the damn pads writing your dumb comments.

Can't you remember what I said without writing it down.

I don't suppose you can because you suffer from CRS and CHS, can't remember shit, and can't hear shit.

I said I feel fine. So you are asking just to be polite, I don't believe that, you are asking to be a tease, you dog.

Family

> For some we loved, the loveliest and the best,
> That from his Vintage rolling Time has prest;
> Have drunk their Cup a Round or two before,
> And one by one crept silently to rest.
>
> *Rubiayat of Omar Khayyam*

You grew up in the country and you are a country bumpkin.
I don't remember where wild food grew.
All that I remember is where the cracks were in the sidewalk.

I don't care what your mother did or how she cooked or tried to cook.

I still don't care what your mother did. She also had you and made a mess of that.

That is just one of those silly Watford statements.

Go straight to hell, you are headed that way anyway.

There you can commune with the rest of the Watfords.

If there are Wilkinsons in hell, they will be there welcoming the Watfords.

You have more of your father in you than you think, always thinking of something nasty.

I know what you mean, you don't have to repeat it, you are Richard Watford's son from the top of your head to the bottom of your feet.

You even look like your nasty father, except for the color of the skin, that is the only difference between the two of you, he was yellow and your are black but the same dirty old man.

I went to visit your dying father in the hospital and asked the nurse how he was feeling?

The nurse said, "He is felling fine just don't get close to him.

I did not know when I married you, I was marrying into a bunch of crazies.

Why do you always have to have someone say how good something looks? I don't ever ask you how I look. That is sad, very sad and very Watford.

I don't get mad when you talk about your son and he is more like your side of the family than mine.

You never talk about your daughters like that, why do you always put your son down? You are he are just alike, no damn good.

Yes, you will buy your son anything that he asks for and give him money when he needs it, which is often, but just try giving him love for a change.

You give your son lots of nice things, a house, a car and other things but you don't give him feelings. It is not in your heart. Try giving him love instead of gifts and it will make you feel better towards him.

Pat yourself on the back, if you can reach your back, old man.

The apple doesn't fall far from the tree, you son is just like you, and you are no different from your no good father.

When did you last call your daughters? I am the one that does all of the calling around here.

Your children are all grown adults, they don't need you to tell them how to live. You have done all that you can do now it is up to them to live their lives as the want to live their lives

Now you say, "Now comes that Alma look." You would not get my mother's look if you were a decent person.

That is my mother that you are talking about, you silly man.

You should be married to one of your sisters, you would know what fussing is all about. You would never hear the end of it.

Why are you looking up for my deceased brother, you should be looking down?

That is another Watford statement, you are so full of it.

That is a typical Watford statement. I tell you those Watford's statements are something else.

Someone destroyed you and made a mess of you.

I don't know who did it, but one of your parents ruined you.

Who was stupid enough to marry a Wilkinson-Griffin, you were, the problem is yours now, not mine or my family's?

Will you? Will you? You are like your infantile mother. She never grew up.

I was not was a Woodkinson, I was a Wilkinson.

You are a true Watford, you say you can do something without ever researching the problems involved. Unreal, that is what you are!

You are right because Watfords are always right or at least they think so.

Before anyone gets married they should check and see what the father is like.

OK and they should check and see what the mother is like.

If we had checked I don't think that we would have gotten married

I still say you don't have a clue as to what husbands and wives do or don't do. You never had role models of either sex.

I don't get you at all, you are intelligent but there is something wrong. I don't think you have any mother wit at all.

I really don't think your mother with fifteen children had the time to nurse you properly, you have tits on the brain.

Try to think of something constructive some time and see what it's like.

Who was your role model? Was it that pig of a father you had? He had his fun.

My family might have passed on a gene for six fingers but your family is responsible for the genes that causes one to be schizophrenic.

Why do you have that stupid Watford smile on your face.

I have been a Watford for fifty-three years and anyone who has been a Watford that long is crazy.

You are just like your father, Richard Watford or better known as "Dirty Dick."

You were born crazy, anyone born to your parents is also crazy.

You can reflect on the way you were raised and I don't think it is my job to change the mess that your parents made of you."

Your mother screwed you up and the rest of her children.

You know because you had a role model, your father went around touching every woman he could find.

I am not a part of your family so I don't have bad genes that run in your family.

I don't care if your family waited until the first snow to make a fire in the stove.

I did not grow up like that and if it is cold during the middle of August I will turn on the heat.

You are one cheap bastard. What are you saving your money for?

You Watfords are impossible to live with.

Put that in your pipe and smoke it.

You are a Watford through and through, you can't go any place by yourself and you can't find your way out of a paper bag.

The only person that you are in love with is yourself, all Watfords are like that.

My family never comes here but every time I turn around someone from your family is coming here disturbing my peace of mind and asking for a handout.

For a man of color you are as prejudiced as you can be.

Your mother really put her mark on you and it was not a good mark.

You are not a happy person. You always look like death warmed over with that no smiling face of yours.

When I went on the trip to visit my sisters we had a really good time. We laughed a lot and had fun, something that you would not understand. We did not spend our time talking about our husbands. Why would we spend our time talking about a bunch of assholes?

I might have called you an asshole some of the time but nothing else and if the shoe fits then wear it.

Life & Living

> How long, how long, in infinite Pursuit.
> Of This and That endeavor and dispute?
> Better be merry with the fruitful Grape
> Than sadden after none, or bitter Fruit.
>
> *Rubiayat of Omar Khayyam*

You will never have a normal life because you are not normal.

When I write my book it is going to be called "Living with a damn dingbat."

No! The lights did not go out during the storm, but your lights went out a long time ago.

Did you check the calendar? No! You did but you need someone to blame for you missing your appointment.

Why don't you consult a calendar it would tell you what day this is? It might also tell you what year.

I should write a book, "Living with a jerk", that would be a real joke.

This is not the month of January. It is the month of February Hello! Is anyone home in that head of yours?

I just ask you a question; I don't need that type of answer.

You would never be able to live alone because you like to be pampered.

It is not so much about sharing a house with someone; it depends upon who you are sharing a house with. I would be content to live alone and all the junk in this house would be gone including all your books. Sharing a house is more about one's space and you like to invade my space.

There are at least five couples that I know off that do not sleep together. I would prefer to sleep alone and then I could get a good night's sleep without having someone always poking me. If you don't like my snoring there is always space in the other bedroom. Try it, you just might like it.

Try living with yourself, it is misery and it doesn't love company.

If you try living with yourself you would be living with a dingbat.

"Help me" is your middle name. Why can't you learn to do things yourself without always asking someone to help you? I am someone.

You used something and don't put it back where you got it and when I ask where it is, you answer is always, "I don't know."

Why are you so much like the way you are, seventy-five and going on five, you have lost seventy years.

I told you a hundred times before, don't "let's" be doing anything, I will do my thing and you do your thing.

It is impossible to get people to change their bad and nasty habits. You are well aware of what I mean.

Yes, there is a hell and I am living in it right now.

There goes that bell in your head, it says let me reach out and touch my wife and annoy her. Your brain is like a tape recorder that keeps doing the same thing over and over. You don't have anything else on that brain of yours but pottery, sex and wine.

Can I breathe without you asking me what I am doing?

I am minding my business and you should mind yours, and stop annoying me.

Some people are impossible to live with and you approach the upper limit.

Living with you is like living in an insane asylum.

You only need me living here so that I can find the things that you misplace.

All that you need is someone that you can nail and a secretary.

Why do you follow me, checking on me and meddling with me? Is it because I am doing something interesting?

Living with you is a joke or a bad dream. Try living with yourself and you will see what I mean.

Have you ever noticed that when we are talking that you pay no attention to what I am saying, unless we are talking about you?

I can put up with your picking at me for just so long, and then it starts to get on my nerves. Why do you have to be always touching me?

Why do you always have to crumple the brown bags so that they can't be used for other things? When are you going to learn to save them for wrapping gifts and other things? Later you are going to come to me for some brown paper to wrap something after you have thrown out all the bags.

You do it your way and I will do it my way, any questions? If you have any questions just keep them to yourself. I said keep them to yourself; I don't want to hear your dumb questions.

I do things slowly, I chew slowly, I walk slowly and I talk slowly.

You meddle too much with what I do. I did not buy that item with any of your money. I paid for it myself so it is none of your business.

Everything that you do is done fast. That is why you will never be able to fuss properly. You speak too fast and keep moving your hands when you try to fuss. I don't do that and I know how to fuss effectively.

No! I have not read any of the Harry Potter series. I don't like that type of literature. I don't intend to ever read them and I am not forced to do so.

Sure, you pay the bills and take care of the house but if I want to complain I will do so.

Teasers are evil people and the look on your face when you do that, is one of pure pleasure.

You just can't be by yourself. I enjoy being alone, without some one asking me where something is or some other dumb question.

You could change your living habits if you wanted to. You don't want the change, it would require too much of an effort upon your part.

There is nothing wrong with wearing a hearing aid, all old

people wear them, so you should fit right in. You might just find that there are sounds all around you.

I feel fine, why do you ask, you really don't want to know? I am just sick and tired of being picked upon, teased and asked if I want to get nailed. The thing about it is you do it because you know it is evil, which is really why you do it.

Sure you are a creature of habit, a creature with a bad habit, a real critter.

According to you, you are right. You are always right except when you are wrong, which is most of the time.

I love living with someone who is always right and knows it.

Don't do things and expect me to be doing them with you. It is like I am on an umbilical cord. I am always attached to something that you want done. If you can't do it by yourself, then don't do it.

Do you really live in this house alone? You really don't care if you disturb someone else.

You said, "Yes" when I asked you if you had money for your dinner and now you say stop at the ATM machine. Why me?

Are you going away and leave these people to their own devices, Lord help them?

You are going to miss me when I go to Texas all right. You will miss me because neither you nor your son knows your ass from your elbow. You can't find anything and don't have a clue as to what you should do.

You said that you missed me because you didn't have anything to write for your dumb book. Thanks and trying to leave first base.

You used to be small; large chest and small waist. Now you have a small chest, a large waist line and a small brain.

Help me with this, help me with that, you start something and expect me to be a part of it, you really are a love.

Living with you is a trip through life that no one wants or should have to take.

Living with you takes the patience of an angel and the soul of the devil.

You don't think of me at all, you are just concerned with yourself.

You have a bad way of asking me to do something that you can do yourself. I will not do it.

Do it yourself and get in the habit of doing things for yourself.

I know I have a problem living with you, I would rather live alone.

When I do something for you I don't go on and on about it. It is just routine, like living in this house.

If I didn't have to live here, I would leave this place. That look on your face, you think that is funny.

You put that down right on the pictures; do you ever watch what you are doing?

Living with you is no trip it is a journey through the streets and pathways of Hell or someplace worse.

Just go away, you have nothing to do so you are going to make my life miserable by picking on me. You had better get out of here and leave me alone.

Why don't you cut it out, you are pitiful.

Living with you is a trip, or a bad dream and no one else would do it. Who wants to live with an old man, set in his ways and with no intention of trying to change them?

Just think of what I have to deal with, you.

You know what you did wrong, so don't ask that stupid question.

I fuss because I am living with you, try living with yourself, try it.

You spend all of your time driving me nuts or asking me where something is located.

What have I asked you not to do at the dinner table?

You are not going to distract me by changing the subject.

I fuss because I live with you, a real ding bat, try living with you and see what you would do. I think it would drive you crazy.

Yes, you used to be considerate, I don't remember when it has been so long ago, and you are no longer considerate or kind.

You are not company so why would I want you in here.

You have limited conversational skills, you can't follow the television programs and I have to explain everything, which is annoying to me. You can't hear what is going on anyway so why don't you just leave and play with your computer or watch Star Trek or that stupid History channel.

No! I did not miss you I enjoy my own company thoroughly.

I hit you because you keep rubbing up against me and I don't like it.

You can go to the shelter or call the police; I really don't care what you do.

You thought, I don't know why you bother to think; it is too much of an effort for you.

I will miss you; you bet I will, with a smile on my face.

Today is Thursday and yesterday was Wednesday and the day before that was Tuesday Mr. CRS.

You are not a husband; you are just someone who lives here.

You don't have to get "Just for Men" to look good for me. I don't need what you are selling and I don't want any part of what you want to give me.

Yes, I prefer country music over Beethoven. Do you want me to say that again? I prefer country music over Beethoven. That does not make or put me in a different class from you or anyone else.

You like Beethoven because it is loud and you can hear it. I still think you should get a hearing aid and you would or might enjoy country music.

What morning did you ever wake up and not think about yourself. It is always me, me, me, I, I, I, and never anyone else.

You have no sense of humor, you are dead. Don't you ever think anything is funny?

I like the way you tear the tissues from the roll, you act as if you are moving a building. Do you want me to teach you how to remove the tissues?

Did I ask you to rub my knee? When I get really old and start to shit and pee on my self you will not be around to help. Just keep your hands to yourself I don't need any help.

I was talking about books that I like, books that I get from the library for myself. You have to suggest that I get Shakespeare or some other crap. You read what you want to read and I will read what I want to read. I am not interested in your reading habits or what books you think are worth reading.

Living with you is a trip through hell that I would not wish on my worst enemy.

I am not a wife; I am just someone who shares a house with a man who thinks he is a husband.

That is the whole story of your life and living, everything that you do is half assed.

You are programmed, Every time I sit at the table you have to start touching my arm or some part of my body. Keep you hands to yourself.

The Complete Book of Fussing and Nagging

Think about it, living in this house with you is a chore and not a nice one.

I am amazed at the questions that you ask, the month is September and the year is 1906. You really have CRS {can't remember shit} disease.

Let's call the repair shop in the morning before we go out, concerning the repairs on the Xerox machines. Well I know who "Let's" is.

You realize that you are a "home body". You never want to leave the house. Whenever we go someplace you are in a hurry to get back home. What is so important that we always have to rush back?

Well you can forget that, we are not going to do that at home or on the road.

You are going to Baltimore to play golf for two days and you do not have to rush back. Stay after the last game and then drive home the next day.

With all the rushing to get back you are going to have an accident.

No! I am not worried about you dying; most of you is dead already.

Yes, I don't mind being alone. I could live alone and be happy. I would not be lonely living by myself. In fact I think I would really like it, not having someone around to pick one me.

Please don't do that. You are constantly reaching behind you to put something in the garbage container and you always miss and put it on the floor.

Sure you clean the house each week when the house cleaner comes. In the meantime who do you think picks up your mess, makes the bed, does the dishes, and cooks the meals? I have a job even if you don't think so. If what you do in that potter shop is a job then it does not compare with the work that I have to do. Living with you is the biggest job of all and I would not wish it on anyone.

What are you after in the dishwasher? Just use a paper cup for your drink.

There he goes again turning the ice tray upside down and now there is ice all over the floor. Why do you do that?

While you were away I went to bed at nine and got a good night's sleep. I only get up at about three to use the bathroom and then go back to sleep. When you are here you come to bed at twelve poking me and waking me up. I consider that very rude and you do it all the time. I need some space and peace in my life. I was hoping that you would not rush back but that was too much to expect.

That is the fifth time that you have said that, stop repeating yourself, can't you remember telling me that.

I guess you can't remember CRS, again.

I am holding up my fingers to show you how many times you have said that but I don't have enough fingers. You repeat yourself often and say the same thing over and over. Its like that one joke that you know that I have heard ten thousand times.

You are the Boss Man until it comes time to do some work around the house. You mention that the driveway needed to have the leaves removed. Did it ever occur to you that you might remove the leaves from the driveway? You just waited until I got tired of seeing them there and decided to do something about them myself. Yes, I cleaned the damn driveway and did the job that the boss man is supposed to do.

How may times have I heard that? Aren't you a bit tired of that saying, you have been saying the same thing for fifty years? Try to find some other way of describing the women that you see. What good does it do you to look at women anyway, old man.

You are always saying that you are in tune with the universe, You are just a piece of shit, that is all, Just a piece of shit and you are not in tune with anything but yourself and that is sad.

I wish your friends could see how you act around the house; they would wonder why I live with you.

You can't move anything without dropping something, because you are not careful about what you are doing.

Most of the time you don't have a clue as to what you are doing or trying to do.

Do you have to put your beer on the top shelf where the milk and everything is? That is the first thing that people will see when they open the refrigerator. I am people, you clod.

Men should never live in a house with a woman and have nothing to do. They become a busy body, you want to know what I am doing ever minute of the day. Why are you getting up, where are you going, why are you wearing that, why are you breathing and why is your heart beating? Go to your study and play with you computer or make some pots but leave me alone.

All that does is show your conversational skills, you sit in the same spot each day at the dinner table and say the same thing over and over. It's seems like you are a tape recorder or something.

Where did you go, who are you talking to, what are you doing, did you shit today, who was on the phone? Damn, don't you have a life, get real, instead of meddling with what I am doing. None of those things are any of your business.

Leave the kitchen and stop meddling with me if you want your dinner fixed. Go to the pottery shop that is your space.

See why I don't watch movies with you, you want to chat while it is going on or you always ask what is happening.

Are you finished with this bowl, if so I will put it away? Don't you think that when you finish with something you should put it where it belongs?

Go watch the History channel and then you don't have to ask any questions. Everything on there is so old, like you, that it doesn't matter what is going on.

I really don't understand how you can quote poems for five hours straight and yet you can't find your keys, your bag, your tools or anything.

I think you have two much useless information in that head of yours.

People don't have to like poetry. You are always talking about people who dance, just because you can't dance. Yet you think that all people should like poetry.

You left your purse in the restaurant and now you want me to drop everything and call and see if they found it. You never keep up with anything; you have the worst case of CRS that I have ever seen.

I talked to Dr. Becky, your daughter. I said to her that you asked if I ever talked to her about your son and my enabling him. She said that you should leave that alone.

You treat the girls differently and let them take advantage of you but the slightest thing that your only son does, you magnify into some giant problem. You are the one with the problem not him.

No, I didn't come to the door of your pottery shop to help you. I don't go into dirty rooms. I just wanted to tell you that my father would have been one hundred and five years old today. Well it is a big deal to me.

I went to the restaurant today and picked up your bag that you left there, Mister CRS.

You always want to use my day. You always have something to do that involves me.

You are in a rut and you stay in a rut, same oh! Same oh!

Just give me my space and get out and leave me alone. You have nothing to say, or at least nothing that I want to hear.

Me with a male friend after you die, you must be joking.

If all men are like you I would shoot myself first.

Go away and leave me alone, I am annoyed. These damn service people feel that I have nothing to do but sit around all day and wait for them, I am still paying for the service and it is not in use.

It must be nice to know everything, and no one can tell you anything that you do not know.

Do you notice how you come in and say do this, do that, no please, no nothing it is like a command? It is not even a request.

Please does not come easy with you does it? You don't have the right way of talking to people.

Who are people? I have said it many times before, I am people.

No, we are not going to open the Christmas gifts tonight. We are going to wait until Christmas day, tomorrow. Why do you want to do it now?

Well if you die tonight you will not miss anything because you will be dead and out of the picture as if you were ever alive anyway.

You don't put up Christmas lights because you are too cheap. It has nothing to do with conserving energy.

We are the only house on the block with no Christmas lights.

My Grumpy refuses to put up lights because he is too cheap.

I hope the Saint from the North Pole brings you the gifts that you deserve. This year you have been good and bad and I can't tell the difference.

The Saint from the North Pole will bring you all the shit that you deserve. I don't think he has enough to give all the Watfords.

I heard what you said. Remember that I am married to you; I know all the tricks to the trade. Put that in your pipe and smoke it.

I would not hit you in the head because it would do no good, your head is far too hard and I think that it is empty also.

Why do you watch everything that I do, what I'm eating, what I'm watching on television, what I'm cleaning, and even what am I doing in the bathroom? I am shitting, is that any of your business?

Well now, WOW! The Redskins are playing Philadelphia, no I don't want to watch it.

You watch football because it is a man thing and you can drink beer at the same time. I think the History channel is on, watch it, you would drink beer and watch it also.

Come on, I don't need a kiss, give me some space, damn, you don't know what it is like to be me.

I see you put the curtains up in your study and put them up wrong. You can leave them like that if you want to. It is your room and I don't care. That room stays full of crap anyway.

Husbands just want to usurp wive's space, and they have no right to do so.

So you know what is wrong with you, when did you get your medical degree at the same time that you got your green masters jacket. You probably got both of them at the same place - Wal-Mart.

Husbands who don't have a job and stay around the house all day get on people's nerves. {I am people}

They follow you around the house and ask dumb questions.

If they are not asking dumb questions they are asking you to find something or asking if they can nail you.

Take your golf clubs and go to the driving range or go in that dirty shop of yours and make pots. I need some space.

No, I don't need that and it would take you more than ten minutes to take your pants off.

How are you going to tell me what I need or don't need? I know what I need, more space.

So that was a good hug, huh? How are you going to classify the type of hug I got? I was the one that got the hug and felt up and down.

I don't want you to kiss my hand, I don't care what the French President did or did not do and I am not Hillary Clinton. I really don't think you could kiss my hand without feeling my tits.

Do you think the French President felt Hillary Clinton's tits when he kissed her hand?

This not the twelfth century and I don't want chivalry as if you know what chivalry is all about.

Oh! I forgot you know everything.

Thank you for fixing my dinner; the Chinese restaurant take-out must know everything about you including your social security number.

When are you going to learn that fixing dinner is not the same are going to the store and buying it? Thank you anyway, that is about as much as I can expect from thoughtful you.

Clean up behind yourself immediately and you won't forget to do it and I won't find a mess in the kitchen every time I enter it.

I have more to do than cleaning up behind you. I have a job and you are my job, picking up after you and cleaning up your mess.

I don't want any company in the shower with me. There is not enough room in the shower for both of us anyway.

When someone get up at twelve o'clock they don't have a morning. Anything that goes on in the morning you will never know about because you sleep through the morning.

I will clean up the coffee that some dumbbell spilled all over the counter {you are someone, dumbbell}.

I will never understand why men are so dirty, lazy and disorganized. They mess up, never clean up and can't find a damn thing.

You turn the phone off by pressing the off button. The off button is located on the phone. Can you remember that? Forget it, I forgot you have a bad case of CRS {can't remember shit}.

You turn the bright lights on whenever you enter a room and then you complain about the electric bill.

No one but you and the rest of the people in that backwards town that you come from calls it a light bill.

Electricity does more than just light a space. So why do you have to call it a light bill?

I know when you were growing up you had that one light hanging from the ceiling and nothing else.

For the tenth time since you cleaned up your office, it looks good.

Please don't ask me how it looks again.

How many times do I have to tell you that I don't want to sit in your lap?

You don't have a lap anymore, old man.

I wish the television did not have the History channel or the Science Fiction channel then maybe you would do things that need to be done around the house. As a second thought, I don't think it would make a difference, you would live in a pigsty.

Living with you is something that I would not wish on my worst enemy.

Money And Finance

Ah, make the most of what we yet may spend,
Before we too into the Dust Descend;
Dust into Dust, and under Dust, to lie,
Sans Wine, sans Song, sans Singer and sans End!

Rubiayat of Omar Khayyam

That makes a lot of sense; you spend one hundred dollars for a projector because the bulb would have cost you twenty. Think! There is an eighty dollar difference.

You do not order me to spend my money on something that you are going to use, that does not work.

You can save all you want to save but I am going to spend all the money that I have and not worry about anything. I made it and I am going to spend it.

You are so money hungry get a grip on life. There is more to life than making money. Yes, I know how to spend money, your money.

If it had been me, I would have stopped and purchased something to eat but you are too cheap to do that. Just continue to save your money. Wait and see what happens to the money you save when you die. I am going to spend it like crazy or your children will do it.

I will bet anything that you did not buy that record for me. I will bet that some one gave it to you or you won it somehow.

You never have any money in your wallet and you always want to borrow money from me. Please pay me back. Anyway, I know where your checkbook stays some of the time.

No, I do not have the heat on. Why would I put it on in this type of weather? The question is why you think it is on. It is just going to cost you some money that is what you are worried about.

I purchased what you asked for and wanted and I will get my money back, just do not leave your checkbook lying around. Just remember I pay your bills for you.

I pay your bills for you using your money it's because you never did it right. Your records were a total mess. They were disorganized just as you are, "Mr. in tune with the universe."

Sometimes you would pay the same bill two or three times.

The next time purchase the flowers for the garden yourself. I do not know why you asked me to do it when you are never going to be satisfied with what I purchase anyway.

You are cheap, when it comes to spending money on nonsense you will do that, but you are cheap when it comes to purchasing something that is important.

You did not buy anything, when I met you; you did not have a pot to piss in or a window to throw it out.

You did not buy anything on me including my tits. You had absolutely nothing and you have less now.

I knew you were going to say that, "How much does it cost to put up a few Christmas lights." You are cheap about some things. Yet you will spend thousands of dollars on that Austin Healey.

You are too cheap to put up Christmas lights. It is not that you are concerned about the energy waste.

You should just sell the damn car anyway. Just wait until you die, that Austin Healey is going to be the first thing to go and you are not going to be buried in it.

You have had that car for forty years, don't you think that is long enough. I have had you for more than fifty years and I think that is enough also.

With your old body you can't get in and out of it anyway so just sell it.

No, I don't want or need any money from the sale of your stupid car.

You did not make me anything either or enhance anything that I had, I am what I was when you met me.

You would be in a panic if your checking account was as low as mine.

So I go into my check line reserve, that is what it is for and I intend to use it. No, it does not bother me to use my check line reserve and it should not bother you.

You have no sense of value, you see something that you want and can use but all you think about is the price. What difference does it make?

You are too damn cheap so you come home between breakfast and dinner and want something to eat.

So you should not have bought those elephant ear plants to put in the garden and yard because you could have gotten small ones from some one else.

You are one cheap individual, the older you get the more you think about money.

You are going to die one of these days and someone else will spend it.

You will not go to Belks to shop, Belks is expensive and you are too cheap.

That is where you fall short; you think that the only way to be nice is to spend money on someone.

You really do not know how to be nice.

I do not remember how much I had in my savings account when I retired and neither do you.

So what if I had a zero balance, I enjoyed spending my money. I made it and I spent it.

You cannot tell me how to spend my money; I will spend my money as it pleases me. When I die, someone will spend it anyway.

Why are you so concerned about money, money was meant to spend. Everyone but you knows that.

So why are you so obsessed and concerned about how much money you have.

I do not know why you think everything that is purchased belongs to you. I purchased those gloves, and you asked, "are they mine:' No they are not yours.

You are so cheap. Prices have changed since you were young, fifty years ago.

Well you do not have to worry about money; someday someone else will spend it.

That is not going to happen to me. I am going to leave nothing for anyone else to spend. I am going to enjoy spending it while I am alive. You would be wise to think the same way that I do.

I purchase things that are useful, why don't you try to do the same thing.

Save your money and when you die see how much good it does you.

I took $20.00 to mail your gifts to the girls, if there is any extra I will give it to you and if there is not enough you will pay me for the extra.

It is none of your business how much I have in my savings account. It is none of your business. Even if I told you, would not remember it for two minutes.

If your account was as low as mine you would be having a financial fit.

I don't have to lie about my account because it is none of your business.

I enjoy spending money and you don't.

If you gave me money there would be strings attached to it, so you can keep your money, I don't need it or want what ever it is that you are offering with it.

Who buys all the gifts for the grandchildren, buys your clothes, which you are too cheap to buy. I do, so shut up about how I spend my money.

Yes, I have accounts everywhere and whose business is it anyway, surely not yours. I am going to open another account at Lowes.

I buy lots of things around here, your socks, underwear and other things. I just don't talk about it like you do. You always have to talk about the things that you do.

Money is made to be spent and that is just what I do, I spend it as soon as I get it.

What is this, me help you pay the bills. I pay the bills each month; I just use your money to do it and not mine.

You are a very cheap person. All that you think about is the price of the item that you want or need, shoes haven't been $1.99 in recorded time.

I love me and I will spend on anything that is nice and makes me look nice.

"Am I in trouble now", that is what the mouse ask the cat while the mouse was stealing cheese. Yes, you are now in the doghouse.

Excuse me, am I not your banker. This man does not know how to do anything but give orders, do this, do that. Do it your damn self and stop asking others to do it.

What's wrong with you, putting your own checks in the bank, do I look like your Kissi.

You can do something stupid like that but you can't take your checks to the bank.

Yes, I am others.

Name one thing that you do that is nice that doesn't include money, you can't name anything can you?

Why are you so cheap with yourself, you spend money on other people, you must not value yourself.

It is sad when price dictates your life. "I can't afford that because it costs too much." Twenty dollars and you only have a few thousand.

You saved your receipts, for your taxes those are your favorite words, I saved.

I enjoy spending my money, why don't you try it for a change. Who or what are you saving it for?

You are a low class person. You see something that you want and could use but all you think about is the price.

It is sad when price dictates your life.

"I can't afford that because it costs too much." Those are your favorite words, why don't you want to spend your money. If you don't spend your money someone else will do it, your children that's who.

I know that you will not do that because it will cost you money, you cheap bastard.

I started paying your bills because you were making a mess of them.

I know you want your moneys worth but I will not watch you being cremated, what difference does it make anyway.

You paid for you cremation in advance because the price went up. Now you want someone to watch you being cremated so that you can make sure you get you money's worth. Get one of your children to do it.

Where is all the money that you saved all you life, ask your children?

So your son buys a bottle or water, why does it upset you, it is none of your business, you cheap bastard.

Are you going to take all the light bulbs that I purchase and not buy any yourself that is just like you?

Am I a financial burden on you? I pay my own way. When we go out to dinner, I pay for my meal. When we go to the movies, I buy my ticket I buy you things and I don't ask for the money for them but every time I turn around you are talking about the taxes and the fact that I got my tax money back. If I am a burden on you, next time you keep all the tax money and maybe you will be happy.

I really don't care if it's May 17, what difference does it make and what does it matter, it is cold in the house and I turned the heat on. It is going to cost you some money, big deal. No, I don't want you to warm me up. Warming me up to you means that I get nailed.

Even if you told me to get it when I went to the store and I didn't ...so what.

No, I am not going out anymore today, if you want it, go and get it your lazy self, I have enough to do without being your "step and fetch it."

Why do I have to tell you when I purchase something, it is not your money. You are saving your money, for what I don't know.

My whole life does not center around money, I don't think about it. Some people govern their whole life around money.

You try to make it look like you are a big force in my financial life; it is enough to drive one crazy.

To you the dollar bill is all that you think about, that and saving, saving for what? Some one else will end up spending all that you save.

To me money is not all that important; I come first and money comes last.

When I go to the bank I put your money in and give you the slip, if you can't remember that, it is too bad.

You purchased this dress for me for Christmas and because it was cheap you purchased two of them. I will bet anything that they came from Wal-Mart.

There is a reason why you always want to shop at Wal-Mart. It is all about money and what something costs. In your brain there is a little message that says spend as little as possible on anything that you buy.

In my brain there is a little message that says, money is not an object, money is to be spent. In my brain it says buy quality.

When you buy a shirt at Wal-Mart and wash it, the shirt shrinks out of shape and fades. After the first wash it, the shirt looks as if it came from the trash dump. Yet according to you, money has been saved.

You did not buy those Christmas gifts from Belks or Radio Shack, they came from Wal-Mart, I saw the tags before you put then in the trash container.

Yes, I wore designer clothes when I was young and I don't really care about names being on clothes as long as they are of good quality.

You also wore designer clothes when you were young. Your undershirts had designer names on them, they read "Net Weight 25 lbs" from the flour sacks that your mother used to make your underwear.

Ok, so they read "Net Weight 100 lbs" as if that makes a difference.

No, I am not going with you to Wal-Mart this Christmas Eve. I don't shop at Wal-Mart. That place is a jungle tonight and I don't want to be a part of it. Did you notice all the cars in the parking lot when we went by, there are people on top of people in there and no, I am not going there.

You don't know anything about the prices at Belks, because you have never been there. If you are not knowledgeable about something that does not mean you are stupid, it just means that you don't know something.

How could you know the prices that are in a shop where you never shop?

You want a list of my contributions for you taxes,

The only contributions that I make are to myself. I don't make contributions to organizations or anything else. You can make all the contributions that you want, to anyone that you want, but don't expect me to do it. It is my money and I spend it on me.

This sweater did not come from Wal-Mart. How many times do I have to tell you that I don't shop at Wal-Mart. That is your store you cheap person. I want something nice and I want to look nice. You don't care how you look or what you wear. Well that is your problem not mine. Go to your Wal-mart and purchase anything that you want, just don't expect me to go with you. I don't shop at that place.

No thank you, I don't want to go to your eye doctor at the dollar store. I don't mind paying for my eye glasses.

Only cheap people spend a dollar for a pair of eyeglasses.

I take care of me. I can't see going to the Five & Dime and paying one dollar for a pair of eyeglasses. My eyes are very important to me and the money is not.

I told you just a minute ago that I don't want to go to your eye doctor, the dollar store. I take care of my eyes and you should take care of yours.

You buy your glasses that way but I am not going to do something dumb like that.

Now you want me to take you to the store to buy eyeglasses. You want me to take you to the dollar store. That is a joke. Don't you think that your eyes are worth more that a dollar pair of eyeglasses.

You know more than the eye doctor Mr. "Know it all."

I will not put a pair of dollar glasses on my eyes because I am not cheap like some one I know. I also think my eyes are more important than wearing glasses from the dollar store.

I do agree that if you had a pair of eye glasses that cost two hundred dollars you would lose then within a couple of hours.

So you have thirty pairs of glasses and they all cost a dollar for each pair. Yet you are always asking me where your glasses are.

I can't believe you went out and purchased thirty pairs of eyeglasses rather than try to keep up with them and that makes sense to you.

I would never use dollar glasses on my eyes but some one as cheap as you are would.

I don't shop at Wal-Mart. Wal-Mart is for people like you, cheap people.

I told you to put the net over the fish pond but you liked the way that it looked. I think that big bird that got your fish liked the way it looked also.

The reason that you did not put a net over the fish pond was not because you liked the way that it looked. It was because you were too cheap to purchase a net.

I bet that heron thought that your fish pond was one big cheap, free banquet.

Now you might consider purchasing a net to cover your pond. It will cost you money and I know that hurts you.

The Bedroom

> But leave the Wise to wangle, and with me
> The Quarrel of the Universe let be:
> And, in some corner of the Hubbub coucht
> Make Game of that which makes as much of Thee.
>
> *Rubaiyat of Omar Khayyam*

So you made the bed and fixed my dinner, now you are going to talk about it until the cows come home.

I am suppose to get nailed because you did something around the house, you can forget it.

Your sleeping habits and your eating habits are out of wack.

Why do you turn on the bright lights when you come in the bedroom?

You do that just to wake me up. You are the most inconsiderate person in the universe.

I know you are going to get back in the bed tonight but that is not an excuse for not making it up.

You are the last one out of the bed so you should make it up when you get out of it.

You didn't make the bed you just pulled the covers up and put the pillows on it, but that was fine, "bless your little heart."

Yes, I am surprised that you made the bed, I thanked you and that is all that you are going to get.

Please stop patting yourself on the back, I don't keep bringing up the things that I do. I always wish you would not do things, like make the bed up every ten years, if you are going to talk about it forever.

You make all that noise when you come in like some bull in a tea shop.

You have your nights and days all mixed up. Why don't you go to bed at a decent hour? There is no use in doing it if that's what you want.

You are a real "bed maker upper." The way you make the bed up is disgusting. I think you do it just to be annoying. Don't try to make the bed up any more it looks worst than it did before you tried to make it up.

What is this business of making the bed and cleaning the house because you love me?

You hire someone to clean the house because you are too lazy to help me clean it.

You would rather pay someone to do it and waste the money.

You can't take credit for cleaning this damn house when you don't do it yourself.

If you went to bed at a decent hour you would not be tired during the day. That is not what I mean, you should go to bed to sleep.

It is eleven o'clock, did you make the bed up, when you got up a few minutes ago?

You have started your bad habit again, getting in the bed at three in the morning and getting up at one in the evening.

You woke me up when you got in the bed, and again when you put the cat out.

You don't know how to put me to sleep, dummy.

I get my best sleep while you are on the computer.

You come in, turn on the bright lights, pop into bed, grab my pillow and then move to my side of the bed and start poking me.

When I get up early in the morning, quietly, you are sound asleep and I do not disturb you.

The meanest thing that a person can do is get in the bed late and wake someone up, I am someone.

You come to bed late and bounce the bed and move around and wake me up and I have trouble getting back to sleep.

You should be more considerate and think of the other person when you get in the bed and the other person is asleep.

When I get up in the morning I tip toe around and make no noise so that I will not disturb you, you should learn to do the same thing.

Are you coming in to help me make up the bed? Even if you are going to eventually get back in it, it should still be made-up.

Why am I discussing this with you, you will never understand, forget it.

You made the bed, all right; you just pulled the covers up over everything. I did not touch it. I left it the way that it was but it is painful to view.

When I make the bed, does it look like it does when you make it?

What shocked me was that you made the bed this morning when you got up, are you sure that you are not sick, are you feeling well?

I have a big bed that I sleep in and I can't stretch out in it because someone that I know wants to usurp my body heat and poke me, unbelievable.

I am someone for your information.

Where are you going with that food? We do not eat in the bedroom. We do not do that in the bathroom either, so forget it.

You are an excellent example of what is abnormal or subnormal.

How many times do I have to tell you that I am not going to call you when I go to bed?

There are people who sleep in different rooms as a courtesy to their partners.

Yes, they live on the planet earth.

Where am I going, "Up mikes, next door to Jakes?" My mother used to say that and now I understand why. My father or someone else was always asking her, "Where are you going", when it was none of their business.

Most people like you have flaws but unlike you, they don't just explain them away.

Yes, the bed was made when I returned from my trip, such as it was.

You probably made it while I was on my way from Washington, D.C. I was gone four days and I know how you are. You made the bed on my return trip probably an hour before I got here.

You made the bed today just before I arrived and look, it is still a mess. That is not the way I make the bed.

You just pulled the covers up.

You just pull all the covers over everything, well that at least was an accomplishment.

I leave for a few days and come back and the place is a mess.

I was visiting my sister, her husband was in bed when we left. When we returned from shopping, the bed was made and the house was clean.

There was not a lot of crap all over the place.

Why can't you do things like that instead of making a mess?

It's my bed time, no! I am going to sleep. If you want to sleep come on in.

You say, "I live in my house", you sure do and it is always a mess with all your crap all over the place.

You have the capacity to get in bed quietly and stay on your side, but you don't do that.

You have to sleep close to me; don't give me that, "Husbands sleep close to wives shit."

You want to get close in bed even though it disrupts my sleep, you don't understand or care. You just want to poke me.

You are in the house, in the bedroom, so take off your hat.

Go away; find something to do to keep you busy, you could have made the bed this morning.

Do you have to sleep so close to me. I don't have enough space and I don't want you poking me.

Why can't you be quiet when you get into the bed? You come in and make a lot of noise and turn on the bright lights. You are a sick man, you really are sick.

First it's wife! wife! wife! Like there is someone else in the house, here I am putting the pillow case on the pillow and you ask if I'm making the bed.

Is that is a question that needs an answer?

You don't go to bed as early as I do, so why should I tell you that I am going to bed. Put that in your pipe and smoke it.

I didn't sleep well last night; you put your pillow right next to my head.

Why do you think that I purchased that large bed? I did it so that I would have some space and you still take up more than your share.

You have your side of the bed and look where your pillows are all the way on my side.

I rearrange the furniture for my benefit, not yours. I don't think things have to remain the same way forever. How long will it take you to realize that the chair and table are on this side of the bedroom and stop bumping into them?

You don't see anything wrong with getting up and leaving the rug like that in the bedroom. You don't even see it as a problem.

I go to bed to sleep and nothing else.

When you go to bed why do you have to make such a racket? Don't you realize that another person is in the bed and that she is asleep and doesn't want her sleep disturbed.

You can come to bed if you want to, just don't wake me up, bother me or start poking me.

I don't remember the day that I came in and woke you up, you come in here and bounce on the couch when I am sleeping. Do I do that to you? No! So what gives you the right to do it to me?

You are really self serving, you come to the bed room, I am asleep and you turn on the television.

Why are you so inconsiderate, you only think of yourself and never consider the other person.

I don't have to tell you that I am going to bed. I go to bed to sleep and nothing else, so just go back to what you were doing.

Me tell you when I am going to bed; you are an idiot, a blooming idiot.

I don't have to tell Santa Clause, the good fairy, you or anyone else when I am going to bed, it is my own personal business.

You have started sleeping on my side of the bed. You do that because you want to steal my warmth or just to poke me.

Need My Space

How long, how long, in infinite Pursuit
Of This and That endeavor and dispute?
Better be merry with the fruitful Grape
Than sadden after none, or bitter, Fruit.

Rubiayat of Omar Khayyam

I can not be comfortable any place around you, Jesus Christ, I need some space. You have usurped every room in this house with your projects.

One other thing, "Did you enjoy my fritos last night?"

Go in your office, sit in your chair and leave me alone.

I had a nice day alone, with you gone and no one to bother me.

Why can't you stay on your side of the bed? I need more space. I need space to roll over.

Move over, move over, I know that some husbands sleep close to their wives but you are not a husband.

I got out of the chair because it is yours. I'm not a selfish person like some people that I know.

So you brought supplies, big deal, I buy things but I don't make a big deal out of it.

Stay out of my office, "You need some tape", like you purchased tape.

I don't push you unless you are in my space. Come in my space and you get pushed. Go on, call the police, tell them I pushed you, they will realize that I live with a jerk.

This house stays such a mess all because of you. I get sick and tired of your junk all over my space.

Don't you have a place for anything? Every time you open your mouth, something stupid comes out.

If I gave you another table it would just end up with crap all over it.

The people out there who think you are special don't have to live with you. Those people would change their minds if they lived with you for just one day.

So you have been at work all day and I have been here by myself, I enjoyed every minute of it.

Why did you come in here, because you saw a smile on my face? I am smiling because I am alone with no one to pester me.

I enjoyed being alone so you had to come in here and disturb me.

Go away! Go away! That is what the cat does to me. I can't watch television in peace; I am going in the other room. Don't follow me in there.

There is not enough space in this kitchen for both of us. Go to some other part of the house until I get out of here.

I don't need any help.

Everyone in the world needs some space of his own and does not need someone invading that space.

You have lots of space on your side of the bed yet you want part of mine.

I don't want you sleeping close to me and poking me, so just move over to your side of the bed.

You don't see me going into that dirty pottery shop of yours and invading your space.

You are always in my office, that is my space and the things in there belong to me. Don't you have a television in your office, this is my television and my free time and space. Go back to your space and stop asking me dumb questions like what is going on.

The Dinner Table and Eating

> Here with a Loaf of Bread beneath the Bough,
> A Flask of Wine, a Book of Verse-and Thou
> Beside me singing in the Wilderness
> And Wilderness is Paradise enow.
>
> *Rubaiyat of Omar Khayyam*

I fixed your dinner and all you had to do was close the microwave and you did not even do that.

Why do you come in and ask what's for dinner this is not a restaurant.

So you feel cold, maybe if you were to stand over this hot oven and cook you would not feel that way.

You sit on your ass and wait for some to wait on you and then you do not wait for them before you start eating, you are unreal.

Tasting the food, is there a difference between that and eating?

Do I look like I-HOP? You are barking out orders, as to what you want to eat. You will eat what I fix or eat nothing at all.

You are not hungry. I'll bet that if it were a steak, you would rush in here and eat. Now, because it is the leftover beef stew you are not hungry. Well, we will have it again tomorrow; maybe you will be hungry then. If you don't eat it tomorrow I will serve it the next day.

I like the way you clean up after you fix your sandwich. You leave everything that you used out…disgusting that's what it is.

We are at the dinner table and there are two types of salad dressing. I picked one and you had to use the same one that I picked, don't you ever do anything original.

No one is going to eat that but you. You don't have to fill your plate, Jesus.

You can't sit at the dinner table without disturbing me by touching my arm or commenting on the blouse that I have on. It is not the blouse that you are interested in.

I always have to clean the table off before we eat it is always filled with your stuff.

Every day I have to clean stuff of the kitchen table that should be on your desk. If you clean your desk once in a while you would have space for all that junk that you leave
on the kitchen table.

You live in a barn; your mess is all over the house, now you are making a mess in the dining room.

You have the worst eating habits, everything is overkill.

How do you feel sitting there and asking me to fix your lunch, no please, no nothing. Who do you think you are, "King of the hill?"

I use the tartar sauce as a garnish, not as my main meal. You seem to think that the tartar sauce is your main meal which is why you use so much of it.

Do you enjoy being waited on, sitting there with your hands crossed, watching me walk over to the table with the food. You must enjoy it because you never help.

I am cooking something for you to eat; you never do that for me. You think that calling for Chinese, Kentucky Fried Chicken or having pizza delivered or going out to eat is the same thing. You are very, very wrong. Anyway when we eat out I pay for my meal, Mister Big spender.

That is a dumb question, you don't cook, you don't participate, all you do is come into the kitchen and get in my way, and then your ask dumb questions.

Are you going to stay in that room and watch the golf game or are you going to come in here and watch me fix dinner?

You don't want to eat rice because you say it is fatting, it is not more fatting than that wine you drink or all that bread that you eat. Why don't you tell the truth and just say that you don't like rice. The rice will be here, you can eat it now or later.

Making love is something you know nothing about, it is not just sex. Just stop touching my arm at the dinner table, that is not making love and I don't want to play footsie with you.

Why don't you take a lesson from me, do I ever ask you to do anything? You are constantly asking me to do something with you or for you. If you are not asking me to do something, you are asking me where something of yours is located.

You don't have to say, "Do you want me to fix dinner."

What you are really saying is, "I am hungry, would you start dinner?"

You have no intentions of fixing anything to eat. Your idea of fixing dinner is going to a restaurant.

Sit in there and watch television, you don't need to come in here and watch me fix dinner. Are you going to help me fix dinner? The quick answer to that is no.

You sit there like you are of royal blood, as if you deserve special treatment.

No one is going to eat that but you; you don't have to fill your plate and then fill your glass all the way to the top.

Why do you have to make such a mess? You come in and fix food and leave the kitchen a mess.

I love the way you sit and watch while I fix the food and then you have the nerve to ask, "What is for dinner?"

Food is what you are having for dinner, FOOD!

You are sitting too far from the dinner table. You have no class, absolutely none.

You will sit in a chair at the table and not move anything that is in the chair and eat with the table filled with your junk with just enough space for your plate.

Whenever you use the dinning room table it becomes a pigsty, the pigs are grunting, look at this mess.

The kitchen table becomes a catchall; all of your shit is on it.

We are not going to eat with all this crap all over the dinner table. I will move it.

I am cutting my salad with a regular knife, it is possible, and you are a pitiful old man.

Why don't you just put that salad in the damn blender? No one that I know chops up their salad like that.

One would think that since I fixed the dinner you would clean up. No! You sit there to be waited upon.

Don't touch my arms at the dinner table, how Many times do I have to say that?

You are looking to see how much I have, why? You are going to take too much anyway, it is called overkill.

You are as bad as the children were when they were growing up, you have to spill something or drop something on the floor whenever we eat.

You have your priorities mixed up; you did not consider that I might be tired.

You could have fixed dinner.

With all that shit all over the dinner table, I have to move it and then fix dinner also.

Why can't you clean up your mess and pick up after yourself.

Yes, it is a steak but that is not the reason that I fixed it for you. If that were the case I would throw the steak out.

Don't touch my tits at the dinner table. I don't like it and I don't want you doing it. Keep your hands to your self.

I don't want you touching my arm or my tits at the dinner table, Lord; how many times do I have say that?

When you make a mess in the kitchen, clean up your mess.

Well, if you are hungry go in the kitchen and fix yourself something to eat unless you have no hands.

Don't make mince meat out of your salad. Why don't you just put your salad in a blender? It would save you some time to devote to your conversation about sex.

You have a strange way of eating; you cut, cut and cut your salad.

Have you ever seen anyone in your life that cuts salad like you cut yours, I don't think so?

You got your bad eating habits from your classless family, you are all alike.

Did you notice how the other people at the dinner cut their salad?

They did not massacre it or atomize it.

That is just what you did to your salad.

It is too bad the restaurant did no provide a blender for you; I think you could have used one.

No one cuts their salad up like that. That is not the way to eat a salad. One's salad does not have to be cut so that one can drink it. Oh, I forgot, old men don't have teeth.

If you have enough energy to get a beer; then you have the energy to fix your sandwich.

Look, leave me alone and just eat your dinner. You are not even sitting at the table,

You should be ashamed to even say that or ask me that, at the dinner table, the answer is "no" anyway.

You did not eat dinner while I was gone. I thought dinner would be fixed and ready when I returned. No such luck, huh?

The dinner table is your time to pick at me and touch my arm and you call that making love.

No! I don't want to play footsie with you at the dinner table or any place else.

I don't want anyone touching my feet.

Why are you still sitting in here meddling with my cooking?

Hey cook, he is ordering a salad.

You come in here and sit on your ass and order a salad.

You are going to leave those dishes there for me to move as if I am somebody's house cleaner. No, you do not clean the house ever, all you do is pay the house cleaner to do it and that is not the same thing as cleaning the house yourself. Anyway, you should pay someone to clean up your mess.

No, I am fixing dinner and you are not. So you are not going to get steak. You will eat what I fix or eat nothing at all. You can have a glass of wine but you are going to pour that yourself.

I am going to eat. You can come in and eat if you want to or you can continue working with your computer. It would be a pleasure eating alone without you pestering me.

That is supposed to make me get up and fix food, because someone says "What time is dinner?"

I am going to warm up what we had yesterday, like it or lump it.

Why can't you come over here and fix dinner yourself, instead you would rather meddle with me.

"What's for dinner?" You will eat what I fix or nothing, unless you fix it yourself.

What you did when you claimed you helped me clean the house, was hire someone to do it, because you are to damn lazy to do it yourself.

You can refuse to eat dinner and watch that dumb History channel on television, the choice is yours.

If you want to watch television take your plate in the other room.

You said you were hungry, are you hungry or not? Why are you so wishy-washy?

When I make a sandwich I don't do that, I don't put toothpicks in it. Do you know why, because it is not necessary?

Why do you look like that at the food that I fixed for dinner? If you don't want to eat it, go to a restaurant or better still fix your own food.

I started eating because I am tired of waiting for you to come to the dinner table. I called you twice and you continued doing what you were doing.

Whatever you are doing in that shop can wait until after dinner.

Again there is no place to put the dishes with all this shit on the table.

I am constantly moving your crap, constantly.

I am not going to eat at this table with all your mess on it. Put your crap where it belongs.

I see you like salad dressing with your salad.

I don't get it! I don't get it! Anyone leaving a mess like this in the kitchen.

Yes, there are steaks in the refrigerator but you are going to have stew. Did you fix dinner? You are a totally inept person.

I haven't started mine yet but you have already started digging into your dinner, ugh.

You are really rude, I am running around here putting the food on the table and you are already eating.

Why don't you fix your own dinner if you don't want to eat leftovers? You don't have to eat leftovers; there are lots of restaurants out there.

Do you ever cook, if you do, then fix what you want to eat?

I am the one preparing dinner so I am going to fix what I want for dinner. If you want to eat it OK, if not, go hungry.

I will wash my son's clothes if I want to and I will fix your breakfast only if I want to.

I don't care if he is fifty years old; you are much older than that.

No, I did not fix your catfish, did you fix dinner?

So whose fault is it that dinner was not ready, are you fixing it?

Do you want to come and get your dinner or is it going to hurt you to get up?

You have an obsession about your weight; I am not going to get into an obsession about anything.

You live in this house and you know just where the refrigerator is. Anything that you fix for yourself is your lunch. I fixed my own lunch and you can do the same, you have two old hands so do it yourself.

I am sorry that I am not eating with you but I am heating my food! I don't eat cold food. Only you Watfords eat cold food and like it.

You can't get to the place where we eat because of your crap.

I could be dying and you would still sit there and want me to fix your dinner.

Your solution to fixing dinner is to just go out and buy it.

When are you going to fix my dinner, or am I the only one in this house that can cook?

What did you do for me today? I might have consented to do it, if you had been thoughtful enough to fix my dinner. Then I might not have consented anyway, I have a headache.

You will not do that either, because I will not let you, I told you that I have a headache.

Why would you eat out of my plate, never mind?

Why not try to clean up your mess before you sit down to eat?

Don't say that you were coming back to do it because you were not. You left the drawer open also and I will close the microwave for you since it is too much trouble for you to do it.

When I come home I should not have to clean up behind people this is disgraceful. You are people dumbbell.

Your solution to dinner is to go out and buy it. That is not the same as preparing a meal for someone.

When am I going to eat my dinner without all this shit on the kitchen table?

You are sitting to far from the dinner table, move your chair closer to the dinner table. You have absolutely no class.

The reason that your knife fell on the floor is because this table is filled with your junk and you have no place to put anything.

Wasting toothpicks with your sandwich again, you don't have to put tooth pick in every sandwich that you make.

Why don't you put your entire meal in a blender and just drink it?

I am embarrassed by the way you eat and embarrassed for you.

Wife, wife, why do you call me like that?

Do you see anyone besides me sitting at this table? Jesus! Why do you call me like that?

This kitchen table becomes a catch all with your crap all over it. Come in here and remove your junk off the table please. Put that crap in your office with the rest of the crap that you keep all over that office.

Did you leave any tuna fish for me, Lord help us? As soon as I make tuna salad you just get up and get yours, forget about the rest of us.

I am "us," you jerk.

The dinner is ready, come out of your shop and eat, if you want to Mr. CEO.

Doesn't that show a mean streak in you? Get yours and what is left is for someone else.

You sit with your arms folded, while I fix dinner and wait on you just like some damn fat Buddha.

You are like a garbage can, you eat food just to keep it from being wasted and all you do is get fat. Yes, I am going to throw it out because it has been around too long. I don't consider that as wasting food. You are not poor any longer; you don't have to eat everything in sight.

It doesn't make sense; I can't sit at the dinner table with all this crap on it. You have your mess all over the place.

How can you sit and eat with all that crap around you.

My mother used to do that and I hated it.

I didn't say anything to her about it but I resolved that I would never do that and what do I do, I marry a man who does the same thing.

I didn't fix you any dinner, how am I going to set the table with your shit on it.

You come and sit on your ass and ask where is my dinner?

If you want dinner you will have to wait or fix it yourself.

You sit at the table like some king and wait for me to prepare your dinner.

I don't mean go out and buy dinner either. I mean get in the kitchen and prepare it.

When you look at something all you think about is can I eat it or nail it?

Your mother sure messed you up.

You don't fix it but you eat it faster than I can put it on the table.

I think I would at least wait until you sat down, if you were the one fixing the meal.

A person who has feelings for his wife would not ask, "What's for dinner? He would have fixed it himself.

Oh dear, I will wipe up this coffee that you spilled on the shelf.

You leave your dishes on the table, who do you think is going to move then to the dishwasher, there are no gremlins or robots in this house.

You don't cook so don't complain.

I will not eat that farty ice cream that you purchased. I would rather eat jello than that crap that makes one fart.

You are going to eat steak? No, you are going to have beef stew whether you like it or not.

I can't get over that, you are going to have steak! If you want it, you will have to fix it yourself.

You don't cook so don't complain

Its my candy and you want to dictate to me when to eat my candy.

You would think that one would move the cup closer to the creamer and not make a spill, look at the mess you have made.

Most people have a dinner hour; they don't each lunch at 3:00 PM and then want dinner about 9:00 PM.

Don't you ever watch where you are sitting, one of these days it is going to be a snake and it is going to bite your butt.

I don't think you would mind that.

The dinner table is not the place for all of your crap. Why can't you have a special place to put your things?

I will take this off the table for the two hundredth million time.

I left your dinner on the table when I went to bed and you just went to bed without eating and left the food on the table.

What are you thinking about, "nothing." That is what you are always thinking about?

You are talking about your taste buds not mine, you don't have taste buds, and all that you think about is food.

You fix your own food this time, I am not hungry. I fixed my own food and you should do the same.

Dinner would have been ready, had you come in and fixed it. You waited for me to do it when I got home.

The day that you start making your own meals then you can complain, until then just eat what has been prepared for you.

Just go away, you have nothing to do so you are going to make my life miserable by picking on me.

Go in the room and watch that stupid Star Trek with all those stupid looking people all over the screen.

You had better get out of here and leave me alone.

Pipe ashes in the kitchen sink; you make a mess of this place.

You don't know what a balanced meal is, all you know is meat, meat, and meat.

Didn't your mother teach you about a balanced meal, no, she didn't because she didn't know what it was herself.

I see where our children got their bad habits, from your side of the family.

Did you eat dinner while you were out; you were gone long enough. I will bet that you did not with your cheap self.

You sit on your butt and wait for me to fix the food. I wish I had a maid to fix my food.

Do you ever think about the fact that you start eating before I get to the table and you did not attempt to prepare the food.

Can't you wait until I have the rest of the food on the table, are you so hungry that you will die of starvation before I finish?

Don't eat like that. You make a sandwich out of everything that your have on your plate. Yesterday it was a cranberry sauce sandwich.

Are you the one doing the cooking? I don't see you doing anything but standing around waiting for me to fix dinner and then be served. So don't ask what is for dinner, food is for dinner. You don't have to stay in the kitchen meddling with what I am doing unless you want to help and I seriously doubt that.

Are we going to eat with all your crap on the dinner table. What do you have an office for?

The dining room is not an office and I wish you could get that through your small brain.

Husbands

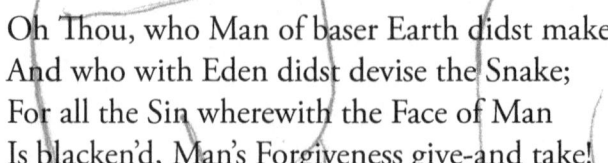

Oh Thou, who Man of baser Earth didst make,
And who with Eden didst devise the Snake;
For all the Sin wherewith the Face of Man
Is blacken'd, Man's Forgiveness give-and take!

Rubiayat of Omar Khayyam.

*D*o you know what a husband does, I don't think so. You are not a husband and would not know one if you saw one.

You want to know what a husband is, a husband is someone who cares more about his mate than himself, a husband is considerate and would rather please someone other than himself. Now you just try to figure that out.

What good are men; they just make extra work for someone.

Husbands don't do a damn thing; they just make their wife's life miserable.

When I die you will marry right away, you can't be by yourself. You follow me from room to room; you need someone to pester.

I don't care what other husbands do or don't do.

I don't want you doing it because I just don't like it. Keep your hands to yourself.

Maybe husbands touch a wife's legs, but you are not a husband and damn if I am a wife. I am just a woman who is close to you, finds things for you and then gets nailed.

What gives you that kind of feeling that you should be waited on?

Men have no business staying home all the time. All men do is sit around the house and ask what someone is doing or ask someone to find something.

I don't want to be a perfect wife; the perfect wife has to have a perfect husband.

If you were to die I would not remarry. I have had it with men.

I hope you understand when husbands die why wives do not remarry. You men remarry because you want some one to pester, to serve you and to nail.

I don't want to hear your concept of what husbands do or don't do because you don't have a clue as to what a husband is or what husbands do or don't do.

So you know what husband do and don't do. Well, husbands don't sit at the dinner table and pick on the other person.

Men are self-centered, witless, and only concerned with what makes them happy. Men have no concern for others besides themselves.

Men don't care about their children or their wives, they are more concerned with their toys, cars, computers and golf clubs.

Any woman who lives with a man knows how stupid and self-centered and useless they are. They always need help, can't do anything by themselves.

Always at the dinner table you want to hold my hand and comment on my chest. That small brain or yours can't think of anything else to do.

The only time that I have a normal meal is when you are out playing golf or we go out to eat.

You are right; men should live with other men in a pigsty. They could get on each others nerves and leave others alone.

You have never had any role models. Your father could not teach you anything because he didn't know what a husband was either.

Husbands! How do you know what husbands do, you are not one, you never have been and you never will be one?

I don't care what husbands do, you should sleep on your side of the bed. I can't even get good nights sleep with you around always poking me.

I know that some husbands hold wive's hands, but they don't come in and bother them.

I don't care what husbands do, just stay on your side of the bed. Anyway all husbands don't sleep close to their wives. Many husbands and wives sleep in different rooms or in different beds. Come to think of it, that is not a bad idea. Yes, I told you before, they live on the planet earth.

Why don't you stop talking about what husbands do or don't do, you don't have a clue as to what a husband is.

You still don't know what husbands do; you never did, when you come up with that love shit it is enough to make me vomit.

You don't have a clue as to what a husband is or what a husband is supposed to do. All that you think husbands are good for is sex.

Get out of my face, you have nothing to do but sit around and call me, "come here, come here."

I didn't say anything about husbands; anyway you are no one's husband. I am not a wife and I don't want to play wife with you..

I hope you are not comparing yourself to a child, maybe you should.

You don't have a wife because you are not a husband.

Breakfast

> Wake! for the Sun, who scatter'd into flight
> The Stars before him from the Field of Night,
> Drives Night along with them from Heav'n, and strikes
> The Sultan's Turret with a Shaft of Light.
>
> *Rubaiyat of Omar Khayyam.*

Did you get up this morning and fix my **breakfast**, hell no; you can fix your own breakfast.

So you are still the King and I am the Merry Maid, I guess that means that I have to fix your breakfast, huh?

If it is not good coffee and you don't like it, you should get up early and fix it yourself.

Are you fixing breakfast, I don't see you doing anything but standing around, commenting on what I am doing, and waiting to be served, Mr. King of the mole hill.

If I move one more thing off this table I will scream. I have moved this pot a hundred times.

I did not make an announcement when I made the coffee this morning.

No! I am not going to eat. I ate breakfast when I got up. The major difference is that when I got up I fix my own breakfast; I don't expect anyone to do it for me.

If you got up at a decent hour of the day then maybe I would. It is lunch time now and you can fix your own lunch if you want to eat.

No one fixed your breakfast, what about you fixing your own breakfast for a change.

"What's for breakfast?" That is what you ask when you go to a restaurant. "What's for breakfast", and then they give you a menu.

Are you kidding?" When was the last time you fixed breakfast for me, you get up late and expect me to fix

your breakfast. If you want breakfast then fix it yourself. You know where the food is.

I fixed your breakfast because I saw what you did to the bacon yesterday, it was burned to charcoal.

I see that you are having trouble opening the orange juice, why can't men open a simple container and open it properly.

They put that cap on the bottle so that stupid people could not open it.

How can you sit there and ask me what is for breakfast?

You are a grown man and totally capable of fixing your own breakfast if you want breakfast.

I had cereal; if you want cereal you know where to find it.

You stay in bed until noon and then expect breakfast, that is an altercation with reality.

You really have a problem, you get up past noon and you ask "What's for breakfast." You don't think that is being nervy, do you?

You know where the food is and you have two hands, fix it yourself.

When you stay in bed this late you should not expect anything from me.

Because you are a male person you feel privileged, you get up and sit on your fat ass and ask me to fix you something to eat for breakfast. I have been up since eight o'clock this morning and you have just gotten up.

It is twelve o'clock and time for lunch not breakfast and now you want service.

You do not have a maid in this house do you? You can fix your own breakfast or whatever you want to call it.

I am not someone's maid. You get up late in the morning and try to con me into fixing your breakfast and then joke about it when you have to fix it.

You just got up and it is now too late for breakfast and too early for dinner, go work in your shop or fix something to eat if you want it.

I think it would it be good if I set at the breakfast table and waited for some one to fix my breakfast?

Well, I eat my breakfast every morning and not a living soul fixes my breakfast but me.

I am not eating; I ate my breakfast when I got up, not at twelve o'clock. The real difference is that I fixed my own breakfast. I never get up very late and ask someone to fix me something to eat, I am someone dummy.

You dropped something. Why can't you be more careful or are you just clumsy? It would be different if you bent down and picked it up but you just leave it there.

I resent you coming in here and saying fix me some breakfast like you are entitled to it.

Do you notice that I don't ask you to fix me anything to eat? It is because I am old enough, wise enough, and completely able to fix it myself.

That is not yesterday's coffee. I made it myself. Did you make any coffee for me today?

If it's not good coffee that I made, you can get up and fix your own coffee.

Get a maid if you want your coffee prepared properly. I'm not a maid and I make coffee the way I want to make coffee. Get up at a reasonable hour and the coffee will be fresh. The coffee was fresh five hours ago.

What housewife, I am not a housewife, I am a retiree. You come in here and sit on your butt and say fix me something to eat. You had better fix it yourself if you want it.

So you put the dishes away, well, putting the dishes away is something that you should do, not because you love someone. Now put your hands on your shoulders and pat.

It is stupid to ask what's for breakfast.

What you are really saying is, "fix me some breakfast."

Kissing

> And if the Wine you drink, the lip you press
> End in Nothing all Things end in-Yes-
> Then fancy while Thou are, Thou art but what
> Thou shalt be-Nothing-Thou shalt not be less.
>
> *Rubaiyat of Omar Khayyam*

No, I don't want you kissing my hand.
Kissing my hand has nothing to do with love.
It is that Watford ability to stir up something and that is all that you are trying to do.

No, I don't want a kiss or to spend any quality time with you, as if you know what quality time really is and your kissing is just so you can feel all over me, so I don't need it.

Why are you constantly kissing, picking and feeling, that has nothing to do with love it is just your desire to be a pain in the ass.

I would kiss you if you understood the meaning of a kiss. You do not, so go into your dirty pottery shop and forget it.

Get out, I am not in the mood for any kissing.

There is a time for kissing, maybe next month or next year. Don't call me, I will call you.

No! I don't want a kiss when I want one I will ask for it.

Why do you think you have to kiss me for the things that I do or don't do?

What good are your kisses anyway and what are they supposed to do for me.

No! I don't want you to kiss my hand. You have done too much of that already.

No!, I don't want a hug or a kiss, what's looking good got to do with hugs, I have to walk around here looking bad to keep you from being all over me.

Try kissing yourself for a change.

I taught you how to kiss and that was a serious mistake.

I don't want you to kiss my hand because you make a big production of it. You get on your old knees and then I have to help you up.

I will kiss you but that does not mean that I want to get nailed, it is just so that you will go out and leave me alone.

Joking

> That joke would be funny if I had not heard it ten thousand times.

> Ha, ha, ha, ha, ha

Into this Universe, and why not knowing.
Nor whence, like Water willy-nilly flowing:
And out of it, as Wind along the waste,
I know not whither, willy-nilly blowing.--

Rubaiyat of Omar Khayyam

You are really the worlds only "one joke wonder," get another joke to tell if you want to tell a joke.

Your joke would be funny if I had not heard it ten thousand times.

You don't think that you are boring; I have heard the same joke for the last fifty five years.

You have some type of recorder in your head. You tell the same jokes and say the same thing over and over. My father used to do the same thing.

He told the same joke over and over and expected us to laugh.

That is six times that you have told me that, don't you ever get tired of repeating yourself?

You are like a damn tape recorder, the same thing over and over.

That same old joke. How can you tell the same old joke over and over and expect someone to laugh at it. It's not funny after the five hundredth time that you tell it.

Now I am going to tell you a joke and I hope that you get the meaning of it. This man and a woman were on a train and it was a sleep over. There was one section left with a lower and upper bunk. They finally decided that even though they did not know each other they would take it. The man took the upper bunk and the woman took the lower. About two o'clock in the morning the woman felt the man's hand on her shoulder. He said, "I really hate to bother you but I am cold and there are some blankets in the closet over there, would you please get me one."

She said, "Well, just for tonight let's pretend that we are married."

He smiled and started to get up. She said, "Get your own damn blanket."

I have heard that joke too many times, forget it.

You are a one joke person, you know but one joke and you tell it over and over. It might have been a little bit funny the first time but after one hundred thousands of times it ceases to be funny. I know what the papa dog said to the little dog after he nailed the bitch, ate all the garbage in the garbage can and then pissed on the fire hydrant.

"If you can't eat it and you can't nail it, piss on it."

Now don't tell me that joke again it ceases to be funny.

You are a one joke wonder, you tell the same joke over and over and I am supposed to laugh and think it is funny. How many times do I have to tell you I don't want to hear your one joke.

So you like Hung, well he is a one song joke and you are a one joke person. He sings off key like someone else I know and he can't dance like someone else I know.

I don't know where you get your expectations from, you expect me to think that joke is funny after having heard it a million times.

You said it once; you don't have to say it again. I am not stupid.

You tell the same jokes over and over and repeat the same things; you are boring and a pain in the ass.

You said that once, why do you have to repeat yourself.

I am holding up ten fingers because that is the thousandth time you have told me that joke and I don't have a thousand fingers or I would be holding them up.

Get that damn tape recorder out of your head.

If you tell that joke one more time I will scream. Don't you hear yourself saying that over and over, my Lord.

You are a person who laughs at his own lame jokes and I mean lame.

You must have learned that joke a hundred years ago and you still tell it.

When are you celebrating your third birthday? Can you remember that?

It's not so bad that you only know one joke and tell it all the time. What I don't understand is why you expect me to laugh and think it is funny. I have heard it one thousand times.

Telephone

> For in and out, above, below,
> "Tis nothing but a Magic Shadow-show,
> Play'd in a Box whose Candle is the Sun,
> Round which we Phantom Figures come and go.
>
> *Rubaiyat of Omar Khayyam*

You can't make your own telephones calls, you are pathetic. You make that phone call. Is this about you or me?

You go along like you are in a fog. I give you a phone message and you just put it down and forget about it. It makes the caller think that I am stupid and did not give you the message.

You don't even check the phone for messages. How are you going to find out if anyone called? I know how you will, by me, your secretary.

I have told you a thousand times to put the telephone back when you are finished with it. The battery in the phone runs down if it is not put back in the phone stand where it belongs. Is that too much for you to remember?

You go to the phone and shove, you are supposed to touch the numbers and not shove them in the ground. This is a damn touch tone phone.

Try to remember if you can, this is a touch phone and you don't have to push, push and push.

Do you know how to turn the phone off after you use it? There is an off button on that phone.

We can't have a regular phone because I don't want a regular phone.

All phones are made this way these days, so just get accustom to it.

Try to get used to the phone; it requires no intelligence to use the off button.

When you finished with the phone did you put it back where it belonged. I don't think so.

In a few minutes you will be looking for the phone and asking me where it is.

You are going to tear up everything in this house, if you are not careful. Just look at what you did with the phone.

You haven't plugged your cell phone in in over a month.

Now you are saying it is no good. Sure it is no good if you don't plug it in and recharge it.

You don't know anything, this store has a public phone, and you are just saying that.

So it doesn't have a public phone, big deal.

Your daughter Barbra called yesterday but did you tell me, No!

I am sick and tired of you complaining about the phone bill and how long I stay on the phone talking to your daughters. I will pay the damn phone bill and talk as long as I want to talk. You are one cheap jerk. You are welcome.

Now you want to blame the damn cell phone, you don't own a cell phone. I pay for the cell phones.

You are going to blame the cell phone for something that you did that was stupid.

Why do I get stuck with someone like you who can't do things the right way? You were supposed to call before we made the trip. Why didn't you call, because you never do things the right way?

I should have taken care of things myself. If I want something done right then I have to do it myself.

You don't do anything right you just do it and no, I will not trade phones with you, you would never be able to use it properly anyway.

Why do you do that, you talk on the telephone and then hand it to me. Just put the phone back where you found it or where it belongs.

Eating

And David's lips are lockt; but in divine
High-piping Pehlevi, with "Wine! Wine! Wine!
"Red Wine!" - the Nightingale cries to the Rose
That sallow cheek of hers to incarnadine.

Rubaiyat of Omar Khayyam

I know you always think about me, that is for sure.

There was enough tuna fish left in the frig for five sandwiches and that is why you left it. It was not because you were thinking of me. I am telling you what you did, old man.

People who spill wine all over the table should clean it up. They should not sit there and wait for someone else to do it.

You are the only person in the whole world who chews ice cream. When you eat ice cream you place it in your mouth and allow it to melt.

Why don't you just eat the ice cream out of the box, anyway we have a bigger bowl.

I opened the refrigerator and what did I find, my ice cream, not in the freezer compartment but in the refrigerator, my ice cream.

Some dimwit doesn't know that ice cream belongs in the freezer and not in the refrigerator, damn.

As fast as food gets on the table you eat, there is no waiting for the people who are preparing it. Would I ever do that if you prepared the food, I don't think so?

I am people. How many times do I have to say that before you stop asking that dumb question?

Why didn't you eat while you were out? If you were not going to eat you should have given me a call. You are still thinking of no one but yourself.

Well, why did you say you wanted to eat? Was it just to get on my nerves?

You should wait before you start eating. You are not supposed to do that at the dinner table with someone else present.

Oh dear, should I wipe up the coffee that you spilled or wait for you to do it. I guess I should wipe it up otherwise it is going to stay there.

You have a brain to tell you that you should eat. Your wife is not your brain.

Who asked you if you liked it or not, this is my lunch, "Don't like chili," Well! You can fix what ever you want for your lunch, just don't expect me to fix it.

I happen to like chili and I don't care if no one else in the entire world likes it, that's their business.

I am not going to eat at a table with all that mess on it. Where I eat has to be clean.

You made your sandwich now clean up after yourself or just leave the mess for me.

You opened the new bread and there is bread in the refrigerator already opened.

That is not right, I am fixing the food and you start eating before its all on the table and I have not sat down to eat.

You really mess up our eating habits. Why could you not stop and get lunch on your way back from Goldsboro?

You can fix your own damn lunch, coming up with, "And I will do that for you," for yourself you mean.

This business of eating without me is a bunch of crap. You just want me to wait on you. I told you before that I am not any one's servant or maid. Go out and hire a servant or maid if you want one. That is what you did when I asked you to help clean the house.

I am going to eat because I have to take your son to the doctor's office, you can eat if you want too or you can continue what you are doing as usual.

Pay attention sometimes to what I am saying. I have to always repeat my self. Get that damn hearing aid please.

I am going to take a video camera and take pictures of the way you attack your salad. I still think you should put it in the blender and drink it?

I showed you how to pour the tea from the container so that the top would not come off but that was useless. So I changed the tea container; this is the way you have to pour your tea, first lift the lid and then carefully pour your tea in your glass. If you follow my instructions you will not pour the tea all over the table and the floor.

Pay attention to your own eating. I will eat only what I want to eat and you should do the same.

Greetings

> Another Voice, when I am sleeping, cries,
> "The Flower should open with the Morning skies."
> And a retreating Whisper, as I wake
> "The Flower that once has blown for ever dies."
>
> *Rubaiyat of Omar Khayyam*

From your wife:
Because you are my husband I designed this card especially for you - So for twenty four hours I will let you be right.

Sometimes it is so hard to realize that you enjoy teasing and badgering me and that you really mean no harm.

It isn't easy to be on the receiving end but I know that living with me isn't easy either.

You are the one that I chose to live my life with. So Happy Father's Day.

I purchased that for you because you are the father of the children, not my father.

No, you are not getting that, father or no father so just forget it and take a cold shower.

You forgot Mother's Day; you did not get me anything or do anything for me.

Do you know how to send cards on the computer that would have been nice?

Aren't you tired of making that remark, always the same thing over and over? Can't you communicate with me on another level?

So it's Father's Day, big deal. No, I don't want to go to bed with you because I don't feel like getting nail.

You have gotten your present that is all that you get.

What makes me remember your birthday and yet you can't remember mine.

If you keep your mind on important things instead of sex you might remember important dates.

You went out and got me a gift after I told you it was my birthday, thanks.

I will bet my bottom dollar that you got that valentine's day gift for me from your favorite store, Wal-Mart. Thank you for the gift anyway.

Doctor's Office

> Myself when young did eagerly frequent,
> Doctor and Saint, and heard great argument;
> About it and about: but evermore Came out,
> by the same door as in I went.
>
> *Rubaiyat of Omar Khayyam*

When I go to the doctor's office, I tell him what is wrong with me and you sit there like a bump on a log and say nothing.

I think that doctor is a jerk, he doesn't like for me to ask questions about anything, my medicine or the treatment. He likes you because you just go there and say nothing, you never question him concerning your treatment. I should really go there with you and tell him what is wrong. I doubt that he would allow me in there when he is examining you because he is a real jerk, like some one else I know.

We women live longer than men because we go to the doctor's office and explain to him what is wrong with us; men seem to have a problem doing this.

So you got the finger wave, big deal, think of what women go through in the doctor's office.

You men really have a problem when it comes to your health.

When you go to the doctor's office the next time I am going to go with you and tell him what is wrong with you. You can't hear, your back hurts, your can't see and you always want sex.

You need an examination twice a day, form the neck up.

"Do I want you to do a mammogram on me?"

That is not the way to do a mammogram it is done in the doctor's office, no thank you.

They use a machine to do a mammogram.

I don't need you to do it.

You don't have any thoughts about how I feel. I go to the doctor's office and come back and all you say is, "I hope you feel better later."

"Later for what?"

The doctor wanted to know why my blood pressure is so high.

I said to him, "You know my husband when he comes in but you do not have to live in the house with him."

All you know how to do is aggravate me all day long, not how do you feel or how can I help.

When I went out early yesterday to the doctor's office, guess what I did. I stopped at the Pancake House and ordered my breakfast and sat at the counter and ate it by myself. I don't mind spending money for something that I want. When you go out, you are too cheap to order a meal. You wait until you get home and ask me what there is to eat.

OK goodbye. You are at the doctor's and you call me to call the dentist and cancel your appointment.

Why couldn't you have called the dentist yourself?

Why do I have to do things like that for you?

I am going to eat my dinner because I have to take your son to the doctor' office. Pay attention sometimes to what I am saying."

I am going to eat my dinner and when I start to leave, in the next five minutes, you are going to say, "Are you going to the doctor's office." You and your CRS.

E-Mail

> I sent my Soul through the Invisible,
> Some letter of that After - life to spell:
> And after many days my Soul return'd,
> And said, "Behold, Myself am Heav'n and Hell:"
>
> *Rubaiyat of Omar Khayyam*

E-mail from Texas: There are 3 more days...counting today and I will be there for you to torture. That is probably why I am missed...no one to torture and no one to nail. At least I don't think so... About nailing, that is. I have so many tales to tell you about my stay here with your daughter's children.

E-mail from Texas: This has really been a learning experience.

E-mail from Texas: There are two more days...counting today...and I will be there for you to torture. You must be miserable not to have me around, unless you have someone else, which I doubt. Old men are allotted only one person to torture and nail. {When they can}

I can't wait to get home and tell you about my ordeal. This has really been one special trip.

Becky comes tomorrow and I will spend my day showing her the ropes. She is very excited about her trip here.

E-Mail from Texas: I might enjoy coming home even if it means getting nailed.

E-mail to my wife in Texas: Your other grandkids and their parents coming to visit today, boy, I am in for it. Sure wish you were her.

E-Mail from Texas: "Now you may be able to see why I will not have another one of our children live with us. I really don't want the responsibility but more than that I don't *like the way they raise their children.*

E-mail from your wife in Texas: You communicate much like my daughter's husband, you sent me an e-mail with only two lines, don't you have anything else to say.

Is there nothing going on at home that would make you write only two lines?

E-mail reply from husband to wife in Texas: Topic: "Writing more than two lines."

"I aim to please."

I love you, I love you, I love you, I love you, I love you.
I love you, I love you, I love you, I love you, I love you.
I love you, I love you, I love you, I love you, I love you.
I love you, I love you, I love you, I love you, I love you.
I love you, I love you, I love you, I love you, I love you.
I love you, I love you, I love you, I love you, I love you.
I love you, I love you, I love you, I love you, I love you.
I love you, I love you, I love you, I love you, I love you.
I love you, I love you, I love you, I love you, I love you.
I love you, I love you, I love you, I love you, I love you.
I love you, I love you, I love you, I love you, I love you.
I love you, I love you, I love you, I love you, I love you.
I love you, I love you, I love you, I love you, I love you.
I love you, I love you, I love you, I love you, I love you.
I love you, I love you, I love you, I love you, I love you.
I love you, I love you, I love you, I love you, I love you.

I love you, I love you, I love you, I love you, I love you.
I love you, I love you, I love you, I love you, I love you.
I love you, I love you, I love you, I love you, I love you.
I love you, I love you, I love you, I love you, I love you.
I love you, I love you, I love you, I love you, I love you.
I love you, I love you, I love you, I love you, I love you.
I love you, I love you, I love you, I love you, I love you.
Want to get nailed?
I aim to please.

E-Mail from your wife: I leave here at 8:10 on my way to Charlotte. There is a wait time there. There is an hours difference between here and there which makes the flight time seem longer but it's really not.

E-mail to my wife: I let your son have $10.00 he said that you would give it back when you return. Being strapped for cash, I am going to need it.

E-mail from your wife: I will reimburse you the $10.00 as well as give you the $100.00 when I get there. STOP OBSESSING OVER MONEY!!!

E-Mail from your husband: Don't think I can wait another day for... Will be really happy when you return. I haven't had anything to write in my book since you have been gone. Took your son to Dr. Nunn, three damn hours wait!!!!!!! I wonder why he can't schedule his appointments so as not to waste people's time {I am people}. No pottery checks in the mail today {damn}. Let me know when to meet you at the airport so that I can make the bed. {Just kidding], I have made the bed every day because I love you and I know that is what you want {And even though I know that I will be getting back in it in a few hours}. Come home soon and get your reward. I aim to please.

The Plaque

> For "is" and "Is-not" though with Rule and Line,
> And, "Up-and-Down" without, I could define,
> I yet in all I only cared to know,
> Was never deep in anything but-Wine.
>
> *Rubiayat of Omar Khayyam*

I put this copy of a plaque up for you, it cost $19.00 and it is worth every cent of it.

The advertisement for the plaque reads as follows:

Common sense {something you do not have} prevails on our decorative and Instructional wooden plaque. It hangs in a prominent spot to state the rules of the house. Provides the most basic guidelines to family and friends {Including husbands} and will make your home a happier and more organized {Note the word organized} place as it addresses the simplest aspects of harmonious domestic existence.

About 5 3/4 x 11 3/4, in a graceful oval shape and with painted raised detail; yours from the artisans of contemporary Mexico.

Rules of the House

If you sleep on it...make it up.
If you wear it...hang it up.
If you drop it...pick it up.
If you eat out of it...wash it.
If you spill it...wipe it up
If you turn it on...turn it off.

If you open it...close it.
If you move it...put it back.
If you break it...repair it.
If you empty it...fill it up.
If it rings...answer it.
If it howls...feed it.
If it cries...love it.

The way that my husband sees the rules of the house:

This is how you, my husband, sees the rules of the house.

If you sleep on it...your wife will make it up. Anyway why make up the bed when you are going to sleep in it again tonight, in about twelve hours so just leave it.

If you wear it...Put it on the chair, or hang it on the door knob, your wife will hang it up. That is what chairs and door knobs are for anyway.

If you drop it... just walk away and forget about it and just leave it and your wife will pick it up. Why should you bend down and pick it up?

If you eat out of it...get up from the table and your wife will wash it and put it in the dishwasher.

If you spill it...It will evaporate, since nature wants disorder. If nature doesn't take care of it, just leave the mess your wife will wipe it up.

If you turn it on...why bother to turn it off, your wife will turn it off after you leave? Wives have nothing else to do. Give them something to do by allowing them to wait on you.

If you open it...leave it open, eventually you are going in there again. Why not just wait for your wife to close it? It will give her something to do.

If you move it...Leave it where it is, your wife will put it back in the place where it belongs. If you can't find it later ask your wife where it is.

If you break it...go out and buy a new one before your wife sees it, just make sure that she never finds out about it.

If you empty it {Ice trays}...Your wife will fill the ice tray so that you

will be able to empty it again. You will also be able to turn the tray up side down and spill the ice all over the floor.

And when you with shinning foot shall pass,
Among the Guest Star-scatter'd on The Grass.
And in Thy joyous Errand reach the spot
Where I made one-turn down and empty Glass

                              Rubaiyat of Omar Khayyam

THE END

CPSIA information can be obtained
at www.ICGtesting.com
Printed in the USA
JSHW051638230222
23233JS00009B/9